THE STORY

OF

MARY MACLANE

BY HERSELF

Introduction by Dr. Julia Watson

RIVERBEND
PUBLISHING

Copyright © 1902 By Herberts S. Stone & Co

Original elements of the Riverbend edition copyright © 2002 by
Riverbend Publishing.
Printed in the United States of America.

Published by Riverbend Publishing, Helena, Montana, in cooperation
with the Montana Historical Society

5 6 7 8 MG 17 16 15 14

All photos provided by the Montana Historical Society.
Front cover inset photo: Mary MacLane, December 1906.
Front cover top photo and page IV: Mary MacLane, circa 1906.
Back cover portrait and page XXVI: Mary MacLane, circa 1906.
Back cover house: Mary MacLane's house in Butte, Montana, circa 1906.

Cover design by DD Dowden
Production and text design by Suzan Glosser

ISBN 1-931832-19-6

Cataloging-in-Publication data is on file at the Library of Congress.

Riverbend Publishing
P.O. Box 5833
Helena, MT 59604
1-866-787-2363
www.riverbendpublishing.com

Mary MacLane, standing, with her brothers and sister (seated, left to right) John James, Dorothy Margaret, and James Whitby.

"I HAVE NEVER BEEN MYSELF"
INTRODUCING MARY MACLANE

Julia Watson

Mary MacLane's literary fortunes have been as varied as her audacious and inimitable writing. In 1902, with the publication of *The Story of Mary MacLane—by Herself* (henceforth referred to as *Story*), which she wrote at nineteen, she was celebrated and widely read. A century later, by contrast, she is often dismissed as an outmoded, sensation-seeking writer of effusive style—and rarely mentioned in literary or feminist histories of Modernism. Regarded as the bête noire of Montana life writing and dubbed the "Wild Woman of Butte" for the scandalous revelations of *Story* and the fame and notoriety she acquired after it was published, MacLane in her young years was a literary sensation. She became one of the most popular and widely translated writers of the first decade of the twentieth century, lauded by Ernest Hemingway, Hart Crane, and Gertrude Stein as an important influence in their quests for a new American style. But her literary star sank in the Roaring Twenties as quickly as it had risen, and *Story* was out of print in the United States until 1991.

Mary MacLane, however, is more than a one-book literary curiosity. She published three book-length autobiographical narratives, and many of the short essays she wrote for the *Butte Evening News* in 1910–11 (several nationally syndicated) crackle with wry humor and complex insights. When a history of the emergence of a western subjectivity in autobiography is written (as it has not yet been), MacLane will deserve a place in it alongside such better-known early twentieth-century writers as Mary Austin (*Earth Horizon*, 1932) and Zitkala Sa ("Impressions of an Indian Childhood" and other essays of 1900 in *American Indian Stories*).[1] Indeed, as readers we need to find ways of reading life narrative that value the innovative experiments in self-making of MacLane's prose.

MacLane reworks the private form of the diary as a site of exploratory and boldly public self-presentation. And her keen eye for detail renders precise observations of objects, places, and people that memorably evoke the texture of everyday life in the early twentieth century. True, she does not fit the model of western writers who express an attachment to place and region as self-defining; Montana memoirist Mary Clearman Blew's sense of being embodied in place when she declares, "I am bone-deep in landscape," is not MacLane's perception.[2] Hers is more an *anxiety* of place, as I have elsewhere suggested.[3] MacLane's *Story*, centered on the place she called Butte-Montana, expresses irritation about the "forlorn" world of Butte with its "dry, warped people" (pages 14–15), its "sand and barrenness," and complements her sense of herself as a kind of "Nothingness" (148).[4] The citizens of Butte may not forgive this prodigal daughter's denunciations of their town or her walking out on it, repeatedly from 1902 on, for the "treacherous" glamour of Eastern cities, especially New York's bohemian Greenwich Village. But, although MacLane periodically left Montana, her writing is shot through with conflicting emotions about it, an anxiety of place that may be more truly "western" than romantic sentiment.

THE BIOGRAPHICAL MARY MACLANE

Surprisingly, no full-length biography of MacLane exists, although Carolyn J. Mattern, Barbara Miller, Virginia Terris, and Leslie A. Wheeler have done shorter studies of her.[5] The contradictory contours of MacLane's life have fascinated some women critics, though most have focused on her life, not her writing, and tend to read her books as transparent self-reflections, rather than the performances of an artistic subject constantly in the making. Readers might turn first to the extraordinary web-site (marymaclane.com) developed by the late Elisabeth Pruitt's husband, Michael R. Brown, which contains extensive information drawn from her collection and research on MacLane's biography, published works, friends and influences, photographs, critical views of her work, and, oddly, multiple personality (Pruitt experienced dozens of personalities), as well as two important collections of her early letters, notably to her publisher. Pruitt's 1993 edited collection of MacLane's writing was a ground-breaking revival of her work that contains several short essays, as well as the unexpurgated version of *Story*, and an extensive bibliography of writings by and on MacLane, to which this introduction is indebted.

When Mary MacLane died in 1929, aged forty-eight, in a rooming house in Chicago, *The Chicagoan* lauded her not as the New Woman of social revolution but as the original "New Female" of flapperism who started a revolution in manners that came to shape both the living and the writing of Modernism.[6] Her rise from Montana obscurity to international fame in 1902 was meteoric. Born in Winnipeg (Manitoba), Canada, on May 1, 1881, of Scotch and Canadian Presbyterian parents, MacLane had two brothers and one sister. Her father supported the family first by serving as an agent for the Canadian government, then investing in cattle herds and flatboats. When Mary was four, the MacLane family moved near Fergus Falls in western Minnesota, which she evokes in an affectionate recollection of 1889, her seventh year, "The Autobiography of the Kid Primitive," published in 1910. That was also the year that MacLane's father, James, died, leaving his family an inheritance that enabled them, in 1891, to move to Butte, Montana. There MacLane's mother, Margaret, married a longtime friend Henry Klenze, whose imprudent investments in mining and other fields eventually drained the family funds. Klenze later committed suicide (around 1925).

The MacLanes lived at 419 North Excelsior Street in Butte, where Mary, at Butte High School, wrote editorials for and edited the school paper, gave an oration on Charles Dickens, and developed a crush on her literature teacher Fannie Corbin. Thereafter, at home, she began writing, from January 13 to April 13, with an afterword on October 28, 1901, what she calls "a record of three months of Nothingness," the dated reflections that became her first book (228). Her "shocking" original title, *I Await the Devil's Coming*, was rejected by the publisher, Herbert S. Stone and Co. of Chicago, who substituted *The Story of Mary MacLane—by Herself*. In a letter the teenaged MacLane protested to no avail the change of title and the omission of her dedication of her book "To the Devil Of the Steel-Gray Eyes, Who One Day may Come—Who Knows?—I Dedicate, with the Mad Love of A Young Weary Wooden Heart, This, My Book."[7] Published in April 1902 (in an edited form that excised some entries and her capital letters), the narrative was an immediate and controversial sensation, selling 100,000 copies in the first month.[8] Within a few years it had been translated into thirty-six languages and praised by leading writers for its startling freshness. Even the redoubtable H. L. Mencken, despite criticizing MacLane as a "Puritan wooed and tortured by the leers of beauty," praised MacLane's prose for its resilience, exuberance, and powerful language and saluted her as "the Butte Bashkirtseff," alluding to the precocious nineteenth-century Russian woman diarist.[9]

An immediate literary celebrity, MacLane moved to New York, where she became a focus of both criticism and praise. She was interviewed by Zona Gale, who contrasted the woman that *Story* had proclaimed a thief and gambler with "The Real Mary MacLane," whom she characterized as looking like "a Madonna and a pot of sweet lavender and a fall of old lace," a demure yet daring child-woman.[10] *Story* was analyzed by literary critics, threatened with censorship, and parodied in popular songs and cartoons for MacLane's frank, brazen, proud musings on sexuality, friendship, and, always, herself. MacLane's literary career of excess and notoriety was launched. The extent of her fame and scandalous reputation were such that the *New York World* ran a forum for reader response, "What do you think of Mary MacLane?" Living primarily in Greenwich Village, with some winters in St. Augustine, Florida, she enjoyed and flaunted her celebrity, making heralded appearances in fashionable places. In 1905, while summering in Rockland and Boston, she led the Fourth of July parade float, lying on a divan beneath a silk canopy as the crowd applauded.[11] She was so well known that "MacLaneism" became a term for rebelliousness in young women.[12]

But MacLane's literary achievements did not keep pace with her media celebrity and cosmopolitan life. Her 1903 book of musings on life and letters, *My Friend Annabel Lee*, was a flop. Her editorials for various newspapers and magazines were syndicated around the country, but did not net her enough money to continue living well and she was reduced to what she called "Grim Penury."[13] From 1906 to 1909 she wrote dozens of letters to her publisher, M. Elijah Stone, protesting that she was reduced to pawning her clothes and pleading, with droll irony, to be paid. Finally remunerated, she returned to Butte late in 1909 where, after surviving a bout of scarlet fever, she began writing lively editorials for the *Butte Evening News*. Some of these reflections on her experiences east and west are memorable pieces, with titles such as "A Waif of Destiny on the High Seas" and "Mary MacLane Meets the Vampire on the Isle of Treacherous Delights" (Manhattan). Publication of a revised edition of *Story* in 1912 by Duffield and Co. of New York, with a new chapter on her life in the intervening decade emphasizing her self-invention, netted her some income.[14] She remained primarily in Butte, apparently visiting many of its seedy evening locales.[15] And she worked for years on the sequel to *Story*, titled *I, Mary MacLane: A Diary of Human Days*, which was published in 1917. But, despite its avowed feminism, it lacked the brash irreverence of *Story* and, in the new realism of World War I, was not successful.[16] It is now forgotten, despite some fine passages in praise of humble objects, such as one on her fondness for "a Cold Boiled Potato."[17]

MacLane also developed a project, based on a 1910 article, in which she characterized relationships with men as "a fascinating, fascinating game" that let her play the vamp and romantic aggressor.[18] A producer for Essanay Studios commissioned her to write a screenplay for the film produced in 1917 and released nationally in 1918. Flamboyantly titled *Men Who Have Made Love to Me*, it dramatized MacLane's romances with six types of men—a callow youth, a literary man, a decadent gentleman, a cave man, a bank clerk, and a husband—and starred MacLane herself in a ninety-minute feature.[19] It received a mixed reception and was banned by the censor in some states; in the short-lived public enthusiasm for vamps such as Pola Negri and Theda Bara, it was soon forgotten.[20] Apparently the sole print of the film was destroyed in a fire and only ads and announcements for it exist today; two are on the website. Although its production encouraged MacLane to move to Chicago, she seems to have ceased writing and fallen into obscurity, as she predicted she would in a newspaper interview in 1902.[21] Wheeler notes her arrest for allegedly stealing dresses in 1919, and film historian Kevin Brownlow observes that her reported attire, a kimono, suggests she had had turned to prostitution.[22] Reportedly, she was addicted to gambling and died alone and friendless.[23] But Barbara Miller, drawing on the research of Virginia Terris, asserts that MacLane had an African American woman photographer friend who tended her in her last days in a Chicago roominghouse. With her death just before the stock market crash ended the Roaring Twenties, her work was forgotten until 1970s feminism brought a revival of interest in early western women writers.

AUTOBIOGRAPHICAL NARRATIVE, LIES, AND EGOTISM IN *STORY*

Story is a narrative of the coming of age of a young woman, a process that constructs what we think of as the "life" of Mary MacLane. But the interpretation of what it meant to be her did not exist until she wrote it. That is, her text is a performance, not a factual biography, as is evident in her fantasies of the steely gray-eyed man-devil she awaits and her musings about the anemone lady. As she stated to Zona Gale, "I pose all the time . . . I have a hundred sides, and I turn first one way and then the other. . . . I have never been myself, excepting to two friends."[24] The precocious MacLane styled herself as a literary character whom I call "Mary" and in *Story* tried out several voices in the process of writing what she calls her "Portrayal," a self-portrait that in every sense "made" her. While Mark Twain dismissed autobiography as lies and damned lies, MacLane understood its strategic uses in creating a subject that only exists when put into language. Therefore, our interest is less in the factual truth of life in 1901 Butte that she portrays—though there is rich detail of everyday life for historians to mine—than in her interpretation of the experience of being a woman alive there, at that time. Where did MacLane encounter the radical notions that shape her self-presentation as genius, artist, bad girl—liar, thief, gambler—and frustrated sensuous woman? One source was the nineteenth-century European Romantic cult of the artist as genius celebrated in the poems of Lord Byron and the writings of women such as Charlotte Bronte in *Jane Eyre* and, above all, Marie Bashkirtseff. Born in Russia in the mid-nineteenth century, Bashkirtseff was raised in Paris and died at twenty-four, leaving behind diaries declaring her genius and expressing her desire to win fame and love as a great painter.[25] Insisting on the unique artistic gifts that distinguished her, Bashkirtseff declared herself the only person who could satisfy her romantic longing.[26] This notion surely struck MacLane, who praises Bashkirtseff but asserts that her own self-portrayal has "a stronger individuality" (77).

MacLane's self-presentation is informed by another literary mode, the pose of world-weary *ennui* developed in the poetry and essays of Charles Baudelaire and the Symbolists, such as Joris Karl Huysmans, who felt alienated from the middle-class bourgeoisie and its European cultural legacy, and were considered "decadent." While it seems unlikely that she read them, expressions of fin-de-siècle weariness were alive in popular writing at the turn of the century, even in far-flung Butte. Like a Symbolist vision of sterile civilization expressed as a desert landscape, MacLane described her setting in Butte "sand and barrenness." And its aridity was congenial to her own cultivation of an interior landscape of Nothing. When Mary announces, at both the beginning and the end of *Story* that she is "a philosopher of the peripatetic school, a thief, a genius, a liar, and a fool," like a jaded sensualist, she characterizes the "Nothing" of her outer and inner worlds as both a "bitterness" and a "burlesque-tragedy" (225).

While several critics have dismissed MacLane's *Story* as the writing of a pretentious egotist, I would argue to the contrary that, precisely because of its pleasure in self-exploration, *Story* remains fresh, frank, and funny. Consider MacLane's opening declaration to the reader: "I, of womankind and of nineteen years, will now begin to set down as full and frank a Portrayal as I am able of myself, Mary MacLane, for whom the world contains not a parallel. . . . I have in me a quite unusual intensity of life. . . . I am a genius. . . . I have attained an egotism that is rare indeed. . . . I am quite, quite odd" (2). This self-presentation is striking for many reasons. It announces a subject asserting her difference from all others and her assured knowledge of herself. In women's autobiographical writing, that is a landmark moment. Many readers have reacted to MacLane's self-presentation as a kind of blind egotism, and indeed MacLane ironically counts egotism as an accomplishment. But her self-knowledge also admits, in the same passage, to miserable unhappiness, lies, and bad faith. Hers is the complex self-relationship of the autobiographer engaged in written self-creation, like Michel de Montaigne in his sixteenth-century *Essays*, Jean-Jacques Rousseau in his eighteenth- century *Confessions*, and Stendhal in his nineteenth-century *The Life of Henry Brulard* before her.[27] All build up increasingly elaborate self-portrayals emphasizing not the facts of external history but the paradoxical truth of interior experience: I am who I am. While MacLane's sense of the contours of that portrait would change over time, as in the 1912 revision of *Story*, her self-stylizing cannot be called lies, since it cannot be proven false—her inventions are part of her, experiments in self-making by one who is, in the best sense of the word, self-centered.

MacLane exploits the possibilities of autobiography, styling herself as a "bad girl" in contrast to other models of womanhood, such as the lady, domestic women like her mother, and the virtuous heroines of novels: "I long to cultivate my element of Badness," she states, wishing for "seven years of judicious Badness, and then death" (162). She states with amusement, "I am a plain downright thief" (102). But even in chronicling several petty thefts in *Story*, including the theft of three dollars from a woman of Butte who could afford it, she makes the occasion of her transgression a redemptive act, describing how she used the money to buy chrysanthemums for an Irish woman she befriended in Butte's Dublin Gulch area (104–6). MacLane's use of confession, then, is strategic, denouncing herself to win the reader's attention and to condemn moral pretension. In calling herself a "sham," a "fraud," a "liar" and a fool, as well as a genius, she shows her depth of self-knowledge and ability to play roles, as autobiographers have done throughout the centuries: "Every day of my life I am playing a part" (96).

As Mary Austin would do in *Earth Horizon* (and probably learned from her), MacLane at times speaks of herself in the third person as a created character both admirable and contemptible (126). In shaping a persona, *Story*, although written as a set of diary entries, has many features of an autobiography. It cultivates a self-conscious "I" and shapes the detail of everyday life into a story of self-discovery structured as a journey that anticipates an artistic destination. Parts of it are related to the spiritual autobiography of interior quest, pain, and longing for deliverance, with a project of redemptive confession, though hers is inverted as a blasphemous narrative of waiting for the Devil. *Story* also engages other modes of the autobiographical: the female coming-of-age story, the story of the growth of the artist's mind, and the literary self-portrait.

Remarkably, MacLane's "Portrayal" of "a creature of intense passionate *feeling*" is a completed book, rather than an open-ended private journal (228).[28] MacLane's literary style is a pastiche of many forms, combining incantatory lists and litanies with manifesto-like declarations calculated to both shock and entice. Her reader is invited to be both sparring partner and potential lover. Focusing on a domestic, everyday world, with its toothbrushes and porterhouse steaks, MacLane enunciates her difference from those around her and traces the emerging contours of a unique "I." For example, she calls on the Devil to deliver her from the tastes that define banal people who like "fried eggplant, fried beef-steak, fried pork-chops, and fried French toast," along with many other "ordinary," "nice," and "pleasant" things (133–34). Her genius consists, she asserts, precisely in her cultivation of Nothing (136). Mary defines herself negatively—not this, not that, not anything, through her exuberant lists of particulars. Both Nothing and all to herself, she remakes the conundrums of self-portraiture for a new kind of subject, a young woman asserting herself as an independent literary presence. Few literary scholars have discussed MacLane's writing at length. An exception is Patricia Meyer Spacks who, in *The Female Imagination* three decades ago, gave a sustained reading of *Story*. She characterizes MacLane as a prototypical woman artist struggling to carve out a space of self-expression distinct from the male tradition that dominated literature for two millennia. Spacks sees MacLane as engaged in active storytelling to shape a self through a Romantic ideal. While criticizing MacLane's "imaginings" as at times "grandiose, empty, self-indulgent, her prose unbearably self-caressing," Spacks acknowledges that what may strike us as narcissism was a form of self-preservation for MacLane in an environment hostile to, and dismissive of, women.[29] Spacks praises the frequent focus of MacLane's writing on the real, material world—her olives and onions—and the intensity of her self-creation. Readers might dispute eastern intellectual Spacks's claim that MacLane's "choice of Butte over Boston," when she returned to live there in 1909 was "the choice of fantasy over reality," a return to a marginal feminized existence.[30] Clearly Spacks had no inkling of the fast women and newly rich miners who walked the streets and haunted the brothels of Butte, memorably characterized in the narrative of a prostitute's life, *Madeleine*, and described in Mary Murphy's study of prostitution in Butte.[31] Despite taking MacLane seriously as a woman writer, Spacks' treatment of her is often harsh and dismissive. She diagnoses MacLane as a fantasizing allegorist compulsive about art and life, "masochistic," "solipsistic," and contemptuous of others.[32] But this rush to judgment may say more about the limitations of the critical moment of the early 1970s in which Spacks wrote than about MacLane. My essay on Montana women writers discusses MacLane as a writer reimagining the urban frontier as a site dramatizing her own anxiety of place, both discouraging her literary impulse with its "barrenness" and provoking her to engagement with its contradictions.

LOVE, SEXUALITY, AND THE BODY IN *STORY*

Much of the power of MacLane's writing comes from her engagement with her own body and the physicality of the material world. She voices self-expression in erotic terms at a time when women lacked visible public lives. At various points throughout *Story* Mary expresses desire for the love of three others: Fannie Corbin, her former teacher in Butte High School, whom she calls the "anemone lady" (29); the man-Devil (she capitalizes the name) with steely-gray eyes; and Napoleon. What this extraordinary cast of characters has in common is that all are remote from both her and Butte, and all designed to shock, titillate, and impress the reader with the intensity of Mary's passionate imagination. Her desire for the anemone lady is enclosed in memories of the past (Corbin has moved east) when her presence stirred Mary with "strange sweet passions" (72) of first love, provoking poetic sensations of music and lush visions (130). Mary describes the romantic friendship she feels for the anemone lady as "man-love" and "a strange attraction of sex" (131). Spacks interprets MacLane's "self-image of bisexuality" as characteristic of the artist and marking her "tragic" rather than "triumphant . . . difference from others."[33]

But according to Lillian Faderman, another critic of second-wave feminism who wrote a pioneering study of lesbian writers, *Surpassing the Love of Men*, MacLane is a proto-lesbian pioneer. For Faderman, the early MacLane in *Story* naively expresses romantic love for a woman, while her later sexual sophistication in *I, Mary MacLane* leads her to repudiate a lesbian orientation as "contraband," "twisted," a "warped" predilection.[34] Faderman focuses on Mary's declaration of her love for Fannie Corbin, the anemone lady, and her assertion of stirrings of "a convulsion and a melting within" in Corbin's presence (96). She reads young Mary's question, "Do you think a man is the only creature with whom one may fall in love?" (131) as a declaration of masculine-identified sexuality.[35] For Faderman, MacLane's disclosure of lesbian desire in *Story* is consistent with the nineteenth century's innocent view of romantic friendships between women, while her 1917 autobiography shifts, like the new century, to regarding them as sick and sinful lesbianism.[36] Faderman, however, does not discuss Mary's major passion throughout *Story*, her profession of love for the devil who is, in her account, a distinctly masculine, steely-eyed aesthete. Though MacLane's sexual orientation seems too fluid to be exclusively identified with either homosexuality or heterosexuality, both the textual Mary and the biographical MacLane are sexually adventurous, with an enduring pleasure in shocking the bourgeoisie, in Butte and elsewhere. And details of her essay and destroyed 1917 film, *Men Who Have Made Love to Me*, suggest that, while MacLane styled herself as flamboyantly sexual, she lived a freely experimental but predominantly heterosexual life.

While the anemone lady is enshrined and idealized in the past of memory, *Story* is directed toward the future Mary awaits, the coming of the man-Devil; her solicitation is a shocking invitation at the time it was written. In the litany of pieties from which Mary asks to be delivered, the Devil is depicted as a powerful agent of change (132–34). Her sympathy for the devil in their imagined conversation of April 3 presents him as the one companion who could deliver her from loneliness. The man-Devil's "fascinating steel-gray eyes" are both "quizzical" and "tender" when Mary proposes their marriage as a bohemian consummation that he, with amusement, defers (206). As an externalization of her unconscious, he both mirrors Mary to herself and eludes her desire, forcing her to continue writing.

The third of this unholy trinity is perhaps the oddest—the former French emperor Napoleon Bonaparte. Mary claims to have seventeen portraits of him that she values for their wildly divergent faces: ugly, heartless, masterly, unwashed, ill-humored, and a host of contradictory attributes (179–80). But he too belongs to the past, though one of public history rather than the private communion with Corbin. And Mary sees herself only as Napoleon's wife, not the leader himself, so this vision of an ideal is less compelling than the Devil, the partner in her imagined future. All of these lovers seem to be versions of an ideal self, powerful figures who enable her to defy convention and conjure a self shaped in dialogue with their provocative images.

Story is also MacLane's narrative of her body, celebrating her vigorous physicality without a sense of shame or sin. Mary's sensuality is suggested in her "narrow shapely" hips, whose curves she confesses she has helped flesh out with "nine cambric handkerchiefs" (177). Her artistic sensibility resides in the MacLane family liver, an organ "fine and perfect, but sensitive" (179). At various times she characterizes her physical self diversely and comically as a "starved, lean little mud-cat" (120), "a little wild savage" (47), but also more grimly as a "barren, hungry heart" (110). But Mary also praises "my fine feminine body" (22) whose organs—stomach, liver, intestines, lungs, heart, nerves—are a "wonderful, graceful mechanism" that complements "my woman's-mind" (23). And, memorably and repeatedly, she refers to herself in the plural as "we three . . . my wooden heart, my good young woman's body, my soul" (12).

Mary's pleasure in her body as her own possession, rather than the object of others' desire, is linked to her enjoyment of material things, especially food. Her description of her sensuous pleasure in the art of eating an olive is justly famous (59–62). Her hearty appetite also enjoys a "rare-broiled porterhouse steak" with "fresh, green young onions" (40) and the plate of "hot rich fudge, with brown sugar" that she makes daily (174). Such everyday material objects as the six family toothbrushes also signify for her the banality of their symbolic family order (88–90). Like her favorite writer, the English poet John Keats, whom she read avidly, MacLane's language is filtered through the senses—taste, smell, touch, sound—creating a story of a young woman living in and through her body and her senses.

MacLane Writing Butte's "Wild Woman"

Mary MacLane is the woman writer citizens of Butte have loved to hate. She was often denounced in newspaper accounts and cartoons as a bohemian "wild woman" for her unconventional *Story* and her flamboyant life, both in the east and when she returned in 1909 as the prodigal daughter. MacLane also saw the citizenry of Butte as "bohemian," but in a different way: as a mix of Irish, Cornish, Finn, Chinese, Swedish, German, African,

Mexican, Arabic and Central European Jewish families. *Story* evokes the texture of immigrant Butte around 1900 as a multicultural melting pot—its back-fence conversations about "the miner's family whose wife and mother wastes its substance in diamonds and seal-skin coats and other riotous living" and "the strange lady with an apoplectic complexion and a wonderfully foul and violent flow of invective" (85). But the conclusion to these vivid details rings with MacLane's characteristic irony: "And so this is Butte, the promiscuous—the Bohemian. And all these are the Devil's playthings. They amuse him, doubtless. Butte is a place of sand and barrenness. The souls of these people are dumb" (85).

Story frequently defies and denounces what MacLane sees as Butte's puritanism and provincialism, using it as a backdrop, "the setting for the personality of me" (13). But the irritation about and anxiety of place MacLane displays toward "this Butte," as she called it in *I, Mary MacLane*, varies at different points in her career. When she returned to Butte in 1909, MacLane discovered that her connection to the town was deep, if ambivalent, and complemented her sense of self. Butte becomes not just a set of specific traits, but an *idea* of place that mirrors and nurtures her idea of herself as a genius of Nothingness. Although it initially irritated her to voice, in a decade of autobiographical writing MacLane's relationship to Butte shifted from antagonistic to affectionate, though she retains anxiety about the region that she valued less for its spectacular mountain views than its congenial social world.

To the young journal writer in *Story*, Butte, with its "good virtuous Christians" (53), was a "graveyard" (15). MacLane denounces Butte as "forlorn" (15), its cemetery typifying its ambiance: "The friends of the dry, warped people of Butte are buried in this dusty dreary wind-havocked waste . . . the Devil must rejoice in this graveyard" (15). Her catalog of the habits of Butte's immigrant citizens with their "wax-flowers off a wedding cake, under glass" (133) and their "regular practices of rubbing oily mixtures into their faces" (134), describes a lively but uneducated place in which she complains of being "a genius starving in Montana in the barrenness" (200). The view out her dining room window on North Excelsior Street at a defunct Butte mining company sums up Mary's view of the universe: "I look out of the window at a Pile of Stones and a Barrel of Lime. These are in the vacant lot next to this house. . . . I feel at the moment that the universe is a Pile of Stones and a Barrel of Lime. They alone are the Real Things" (182–83). In Mary's mirror relationship to her Butte surroundings, it is "the picture of me in *my* sand and barrenness" (139, emphasis added).

As a writer's landscape, however, Butte is sympathetic as well as antagonistic: "Butte and its immediate vicinity present as ugly an outlook as one could wish to see. It is so ugly indeed that it is near the perfection of ugliness. And anything perfect, or nearly so, is not to be despised. I have reached some astonishing subtleties of conception as I have walked for miles over the sand and barrenness among the little hills and gulches. Their utter desolateness is an inspiration to the long, long thoughts and to the nameless wanting." If, like her life, Butte is "an empty damned weariness," it is also an inspiringly diverse locale (12). MacLane asks, "For mixture, for miscellany—variedness, Bohemianism—where is Butte's rival?" (80)

After *Story*, MacLane increasingly acknowledged Butte's importance to her self-conception. She confides in the interview with Zona Gale, "When I wrote my book . . . I hated Butte. I hated the sand and the barrenness. I hated the people and the life. Now I know I should love to go back there and live there. I know that I love Butte. I didn't at nineteen. I do at twenty-one."[37] After returning to Butte, MacLane also professed her attachment to it in her *Butte Evening News* pieces. In "The Borrower of Two-Dollar Bills—and Other Women," she states: "When you come right down to it, I am fond of those gay buccaneers, the citizens of Butte, whose victims are the set-apart individualities in their midst."[38]

And in "The Second *Story of Mary MacLane*" (1910) she extensively traces the history of her relationship to Butte, acknowledging she was "pre-eminently a Butte product—a shy and delicate creature born of this convulsive desolation."[39] After her "wailing" at Butte in *Story* and experience of its curses in response, MacLane claims, seven years later "something in Butte subtly called me. I have heart-feelings for it. These barren hills saw my mind's awakening. . . . A certain deadly thrall hangs over this little place, which impregnates one's mind if one happens to possess one—they're rare—and brings it to a reckoning . . . . It has an exquisite forlornness."[40] MacLane sums up her changed feeling for Butte thus: "The thing I took away with me from Butte seven years ago—a restlessness of spirit, a shadowed and turbulent mentality, a lack of inward peace—is the thing I've brought back with me . . . I am myself like this little town with its subtle deadly thrall upon it, yet fired with certain headlong madnesses of youth." Observing the "outward deadlock of this semi-bewitched Butte," she declares her allegiance to "the darksome spirit of Butte-Montana hard and fast upon me" . . . "I am once more a citizen of Butte."[41]

Comparing Butte to her other home, New York City's Greenwich Village, where she spent several years after the publication of *Story*, MacLane contrasts her two "Bohemian" environments in "Mary MacLane Meets the Vampire on the Isle of Treacherous Delights." New York is characterized as "the vampire, the cruel and much-loved" place that fills her with "a half-insane emotion of far desire."[42] As a vampire it devours but offers vivid, restless life until it drains its lovers: "The quality that is so distinctively New Yorkish, and which Butte-Montana conspicuously lacks . . . is the quality of deep and intimate humanness."[43] This urbane warmth, both intoxicating and "nerve-racking," is the opposite of the texture of life in Butte, MacLane asserts: "Since I've been gone from it I realize that the people in Butte are all abnormal in that they form no real intimacies. They are as shy as wild seafowl with each other, and absolutely dead-locked in iron-bound personal isolation. They have what they call friendships . . . but . . . they are not, they seemingly can't be, intimate with each other. They think they exchange bits of their personalities, when they are really exchanging only talk. . . . I idly wonder as I sit here whether there would be anything intimate about even the doing of a murder in Butte."[44] Despite the "wild sea-bird shyness" that characterizes Butte for MacLane, she denounces its conventionality as a place where "on-lookers make scarlet mountains of drab mole hills."[45] Ambivalent about her "Bohemian" worlds both east and west, MacLane nonetheless finally acknowledges Butte's charm: "Butte is sordid, beastly and time-serving—but withal full of romance and poetry and the wideness of the west." [46]

In returning to Butte, MacLane found that the town had imagined her as its bad girl or "wild woman." In "The Autobiography of the Kid Primitive," MacLane decries the hostility the citizens of Butte directed at her in contrast to her fond recollection of childhood in Fergus Falls. Ironically, her perceived egotism both condemned her and made her columns a great read. "If I seem mostly to write about myself for the citizens of Butte to run and read, it is not because of egotism and vanity . . . [if I] write for the *Evening News* about such things as the condition of the roads, or the height of the Big Butte, or the look of the highlands, or the color of the sunsets— . . . the people who condemn me for egotism and all will be the first to cease reading."[47] MacLane sensed that her notoriety had endeared her to Butte as the writer its readers loved to hate.

THE ENDURING SIGNIFICANCE OF MARY MACLANE

MacLane was an exceptional woman in taking herself seriously as a writer and public figure at a time, in the early twentieth century, when relatively few women who aspired to become artists dared question the boundaries of decorum and domesticity. Unlike her contemporaries—the aristocratic Edith Wharton, social reformers Ida B. Wells and Jane Addams, or women who wrote from the security of their family homes— MacLane fashioned an impudent autobiographical "I" that spoke to an emerging Modernist sensibility. Her narratives created an adventurous, if melodramatic, character who challenged traditional limits of middle-class white women's lives and enjoyed—indeed flaunted—her own celebrity and defiance of convention. And, unlike many women who aspired to lead independent, liberated lives before the success of women's suffrage in 1920, MacLane made herself into a professional writer despite her lack of education and mentoring. Her narratives, above all, *Story*, are stirring portraits of what it meant to be alive—and a woman desirous of being less marginal, more alive—at the start of the twentieth century.

In her deeply ambivalent relationship to her western roots MacLane seems to have internalized Butte's enterprising, assertive character while deploring the smug provinciality of the town's upstanding citizens. Despite her attraction to the dash and elegance of eastern cities, she nurtured a restless desire for raw, fresh experience that Butte's rough character offered and that increasingly eluded her in middle age. MacLane is both exceptional to *and* representative of western women at the turn of the century. In contrast to more frequently read Montana women writers such as Nannie Alderson, a rancher's wife who immigrated from the East, MacLane grew up in emerging western towns.[48] She composed her own narrative rather than telling it to an interlocutor (as Alderson did in *A Bride Goes West*) and wrote it as a passionate young woman hungry for a different world rather than in middle-aged retrospection. As a professional writer she articulated an unconventional critique of the West informed both by urban eastern worldliness and European literary tastes. MacLane's West is not the frontier landscape of western novels and her focus not an environmentalist's view of the land. But in writing Butte as a place of both "sand and barrenness" and bustling immigrant diversity, she gives new meaning to the inland Rockies as origin and home. Clearly, MacLane's desire to escape Butte was linked to her lifelong mental inhabiting of it and her sense of being part of its diverse, rollicking community. As she, at the conclusion of "The Autobiography of the Kid Primitive," urges "the gay buccaneers of Butte" to salute her and "mix. . . a mental cocktail—of the gin of introspect, the vermouth of retrospect, and the subtle bitter of unshed tears," we too might drink to her accomplishment in memorializing all of them.[49]

ABOUT JULIA WATSON

Julia Watson is an associate professor in the Department of Comparative Studies at The Ohio State University and was previously the first director of the Women's Studies Program at the University of Montana and chair of the Department of Women's Studies at California State University-Northridge. With Sidonie Smith she has co-written *Reading Autobiography: A Guide for Interpreting Life Narratives* (2001) and co-edited four collections of essays: *De/Colonizing the Subject: The Politics of Gender in Women's Autobiography* (1992), *Getting a Life: Everyday Uses of Autobiography* (1996), *Women, Autobiography, Theory: A Reader* (1998), and *Interfaces: Women, Autobiography, Image, Performance* (2002). Her most recent essays are on the autobiographical painter Charlotte Salomon and writer Janet Campbell Hale.

NOTES

I am grateful to Mary Murphy and Margaret Kingsland for encouraging my interest in Mary MacLane, and to the 1996 "Only in Butte," Montana Historical Society Conference organizers, and particularly Martha Kohl for opportunities to write about her.

1. Mary Austin, *Earth Horizon: Autobiography,* ed. 1991, ed. Melodie Graulich (1932; Albuquerque, N.Mex., 1991); Zitkala Sa, *American Indian Stories* (Washington, D.C., 1921).

2. Mary Clearman Blew, *All But the Waltz: A Memoir of Five Generations in the Life of a Montana Family* (New York, 1991), 7.

3. Julia Watson, "Engendering Montana Lives: Women's Autobiographical Writing," in *Writing Montana: Literature under the Big Sky*, ed. Rick Newby and Suzanne Hunger (Helena, Mont., 1996), 141–42.

4. Parenthetical page numbers refer to the location of the quotations in this edition.

5. Carolyn J. Mattern, "Mary MacLane: A Feminist Opinion," *Montana The Magazine of Western History*, 27 (Autumn 1977), 54–63; Barbara Miller, "'Hot as Live Embers—Cold as Hail': The Restless Soul of Butte's Mary MacLane," *Montana Magazine*, September 1982, 50–53; Virginia Terris, "Mary MacLane—Realist," *The Speculator*, Summer 1985, 42–49; Leslie A. Wheeler, "Montana's Shocking 'Lit'ry Lady'," *Montana The Magazine of Western History*, 27 (Summer 1977), 20–33.

6. In its eulogy, *The Chicagoan* asked: "How did it happen that a revolution in manners, a transvaluation of values in the female code of behavior, started, or seemed to start, with an unruly young woman who couldn't bear the sight of

the tooth-brush in the family bathroom at Butte, Montana? What seed fell upon that austere provincial soil to produce this amorous diarist with a narcissus complex? What mystic or glandular voices spoke to Mary, bidding her go forth into the world as the Jeanne d'Arc of the Warm Mammas?" The Chicagoan, August 31, 1929, quoted in Elizabeth Pruitt, ed., *Tender Darkness: A Mary MacLane Anthology* (Belmont, Calif., 1993), viii.

7. Ibid., 191–92.

8. Ibid., vii.

9. H.L. Mencken, "The Butte Bashkirtseff," in *Prejudices: First Series* (New York, 1919), 123.

10. Zona Gale, "The Real Mary MacLane," *New York World*, August 17, 1902, reprinted in Pruitt, *Tender Darkness*, 128.

11. Robert Taylor, "Bookmaking," *Boston Globe*, August 7, 1994.

12. Wheeler, "Montana's Shocking 'Lit'ry Lady'," 26.

13. Mary MacLane to M. Elijah Stone, December 24, 1906, Michael R. Brown's personal web site, http://www.marymaclane.com/mary/works/letters/stone.html.

14. Patricia Meyer Spacks, *The Female Imagination* (1975; reprint, New York, 1976), 224.

15. Mattern, "Mary MacLane," 63.

16. On the feminism of *I, Mary MacLane*, see ibid., 61.

17. Mary MacLane, "God Compensates Me," in *The Last Best Place: A Montana Anthology*, ed. William Kittredge and Annick Smith (1988; reprint, Seattle, 1991), 487–88.

18. Mattern, "Mary MacLane," 61–63.

19. Brownlow points out that, at the time, "the euphemism 'making love' did not apply solely to coitus, as it does now, but referred to any romantic approach." Kevin Brownlow, *Behind the Mask of Innocence: Sex, Violence and Crime—Films of Social Conscience in the Silent Era* (New York, 1990), 30.

20. Ibid., 30–32.

21. Gale, "The Real Mary MacLane," 131–32.

22. Wheeler, "Montana's Shocking 'Lit'ry Lady'," 33; Brownlow, *Behind the Mask of Innocence*, 515, n.31.

23. Brownlow, *Behind the Mask of Innocence*, 32.

24. Gale, "The Real Mary MacLane," 130–31.

25. Marie Bashkirtseff, *The Journal of Marie Bashkirtseff*, trans. Mathilde Blind (1890; reprint, London, 1985).

26. Spacks, *The Female Imagination*, 216–19.

27. Michel de Montaigne, *The Complete Essays of Montaigne*, trans. Donald M. Frame (Stanford, Calif., 1958); Jean-Jacques Rousseau, *Confessions* (Hertfordshire, U.K., 1996); Stendhal [Henri Beyle], *The Life of Henry Brulard*, trans. Jean Stewart and B. C. J. G. Knight (New York, 1968).

28. As life writing theorist Philippe Lejeune has noted, most journals, even Bashkirtseff's, remain largely unpublished. It is "a very immediate form of

writing and marked by distress." And the journal is a practice, a way of life that follows some threads but not the whole fabric of a life, though even the most private journal is addressed to an imaginary reader, "motivated by a search for communication." MacLane's desire for a full portrayal of herself exceeds the limits of journal-writing and launches her as a published artist. Philippe Lejeune, "The Practice of the Private Journal: Chronicle of an Investigation (1986–1998)," in *Marginal Voices, Marginal Forms: Diaries in European Literature and History*, ed. Rachael Langford and Russell West (Amsterdam, 1999), 185, 187, 192.

29. Spacks, *The Female Imagination*, 225, 406.

30. Ibid., 227.

31. *Madeleine: An Autobiography* (1919; reprint, New York, 1986); Mary Murphy, "The Private Lives of Public Women: Prostitution in Butte, Montana, 1878–1917," in *The Women's West*, ed. Susan Armitage and Elizabeth Jameson (Norman, Okla., 1987), 193–205.

32. Spacks, *The Female Imagination*, 228, 231.

33. Ibid., 223.

34. Quoted in Lillian Faderman, *Surpassing the Love of Men: Romantic Friendship and Love Between Women from the Renaissance to the Present* (New York, 1981), 299–300.

35. Ibid., 299.

36. Ibid.

37. Gale, "The Real Mary MacLane," 129.

38. Mary MacLane, "The Borrower of Two-Dollar Bills—and Other Women," *Butte (Mont.) Evening News*, May 15, 1910, reprinted in Pruitt, *Tender Darkness*, 162.

39. Mary MacLane, "The Second *Story of Mary MacLane*," *Butte (Mont.) Evening News*, January 23, 1910, reprinted in Pruitt, *Tender Darkness*, 150.

40. Ibid.

41. Ibid., 154.

42. Mary MacLane, "Mary MacLane Meets the Vampire on the Isle of Treacherous Delights," *Butte (Mont.) Evening News*, March 27, 1910, reprinted in Pruitt, *Tender Darkness*, 155.

43. Ibid., 157.

44. Ibid., 158.

45. Ibid., 159.

46. Ibid., 149–50.

47. Mary MacLane, "The Autobiography of the Kid Primitive," *Butte (Mont.) Evening News*, April 3, 1910, reprinted in Pruitt, *Tender Darkness*, 178–79.

48. Nannie T. Alderson and Helena Huntington Smith, *A Bride Goes West* (1942; reprint, Lincoln, Neb., 1969).

49. MacLane, "The Autobiography of the Kid Primitive," 187.

Mary MacLane

THE STORY OF MARY MACLANE

I OF womankind and of nineteen years, will now begin to set down as full and frank a Portrayal as I am able of myself, Mary MacLane, for whom the world contains not a parallel.

I am convinced of this, for I am odd.

I am distinctly original innately and in development.

I have in me a quite unusual intensity of life.

I can feel.

I have a marvelous capacity for misery and for happiness.

I am broad-minded.

I am a genius.

I am a philosopher of my own good peripatetic school.

I care neither for right nor for wrong—my conscience is nil.

My brain is a conglomeration of aggressive versatility.

I have reached a truly wonderful state of miserable morbid happiness.

I know myself, oh, very well.

I have gone into the deep shadows.

1

All this constitutes oddity. I find, therefore, that I am quite, quite odd.

I have hunted for even the suggestion of a parallel among the several hundred persons that I call acquaintances. But in vain. There are people and people of varying depths and intricacies of character, but there is none to compare with me. The young ones of my own age—if I chance to give them but a glimpse of the real workings of my mind—can only stare at me in dazed stupidity, uncomprehending; and the old ones of forty and fifty—for forty and fifty are always old to nineteen—can but either stare also in stupidity, or else, their own narrowness asserting itself, smile their little devilish smile of superiority which they reserve indiscriminately for all foolish young things. The utter idiocy of forty and fifty at times!

These, to be sure, are extreme instances. There are among my young acquaintances some who do not stare in stupidity, and yes, even at forty and fifty there are some who understand some phases of my complicated character, though none to comprehend it in its entirety.

But, as I said, even the suggestion of a parallel is not to be found among them.

I think at this moment, however, of two minds famous in the world of letters between which and mine there are certain fine points of similarity.

These are the minds of Lord Byron and of Marie Bashkirtseff. It is the Byron of "Don Juan" in whom I find suggestions of myself. In this sublime outpouring there are few to admire the character of Don Juan, but all must admire Byron. He is truly admirable. He uncovered and exposed his soul of mingled good and bad—as the terms are—for the world to gaze upon. He knew the human race, and he knew himself.

As for that strange notable, Marie Bashkirtseff, yes, I am rather like her in many points, as I've been told. But in most things I go beyond her.

Where she is deep, I am deeper.

Where she is wonderful in her intensity, I am still more wonderful in my intensity.

Where she had philosophy, I am a philosopher.

Where she had astonishing vanity and conceit, I have yet more astonishing vanity and conceit.

But she, forsooth, could paint good pictures,—and I—what can I do?

She had a beautiful face, and I am a plain-featured, insignificant little animal.

She was surrounded by admiring, sympathetic friends, and I am alone—alone, though there are people and people.

She was a genius, and still more am I a genius.

She suffered with the pain of a woman, young; and I suffer with the pain of a woman, young and all alone.

And so it is.

Along some lines I have gotten to the edge of the world. A step more and I fall off. I do not take the step. I stand on the edge, and I suffer.

Nothing, oh, nothing on the earth can suffer like a woman young and all alone!

—Before proceeding farther with the Portraying of Mary MacLane, I will write out some of her uninteresting history.

I was born in 1881 at Winnepeg, in Canada. Whether Winnepeg will yet live to be proud of this fact is a matter for some conjecture and anxiety on my part. When I was four years old I was taken with my family to a little town in western Minnesota, where I lived a more or less vapid and lonely life until I was ten. We came then to Montana.

Whereat the aforesaid life was continued.

My father died when I was eight. Apart from feeding and clothing me comfortably and sending me to School—which is no more than was due me—and transmitting to me the MacLane blood and character, I can not see that he ever gave me a single thought. Certainly he did not love me, for he was quite incapable of loving any one but himself. And since nothing is of any moment in this world without the love of human beings for each other, it is a matter of supreme indifference to me whether my father, Jim MacLane of selfish memory, lived or died.

He is nothing to me.

There are with me still a mother, a sister, and two brothers.

They also are nothing to me.

They do not understand me any more than if I were some strange live curiosity, as which I dare say they regard me.

I am peculiarly of the MacLane blood, which is Highland Scotch. My sister and brothers inherit the traits of their mother's family, which is of Scotch Lowland descent. This alone makes no small degree of difference. Apart from this the MacLanes—these particular MacLanes—are just a little bit different from every family in Canada, and from every other that I've known. It contains and has contained fanatics of many minds—religious, social, whatnot, and I am a true MacLane.

There is absolutely no sympathy between my immediate family and me. There can never be. My mother, having been with me during the whole of my nineteen years, has an utterly distorted idea of my nature and its desires, if indeed she has any idea of it.

When I think of the exquisite love and sympathy which might be between a mother and daughter, I feel myself defrauded of a beautiful thing rightfully mine, in a world where for me such things are pitiably few.

It will always be so.

My sister and brothers are not interested in me and my analyses and philosophy, and my wants. Their own are strictly practical and material. The love and sympathy between human beings is to them, it seems, a thing only for people in books.

In short, they are Lowland Scotch, and I am a MacLane.

And so, as I've said, I carried my uninteresting existence into Montana. The existence became less uninteresting, however, as my versatile mind began to develop and grow and know the glittering things that are. But I realized as the years were passing that my own life was at best a vapid, negative thing.

A thousand treasures that I wanted were lacking.

I graduated from the high school with these things: very good Latin; good French and Greek; indifferent geometry and other mathematics; a broad conception of history and literature; peripatetic philosophy that I acquired without any aid from the high school; genius of a kind, that has always been with me; an empty heart that has taken on a certain wooden quality; an excellent strong young woman's-body; a pitiably starved soul.

With this equipment I have gone my way through the last two years. But my life, though unsatisfying and warped, is no longer insipid. It is fraught with a poignant misery—the misery of nothingness.

I have no particular thing to occupy me. I write every day. Writing is a necessity—like eating. I do a little housework, and on the whole I am rather fond of it—some parts of it. I dislike dusting chairs, but I have no aversion to scrubbing floors. Indeed, I have gained much of my strength and gracefulness of body from scrubbing the kitchen floor—to say nothing of some fine points of philosophy. It brings a certain energy to one's body and to one's brain.

But mostly I take walks far away in the open country. Butte and its immediate vicinity present as ugly an outlook as one could wish to see. It is so ugly indeed that it is near the perfection of ugliness. And anything perfect, or nearly so, is not to be despised. I have reached some astonishing subtleties of conception as I have walked for miles over the sand and barrenness among the little hills and gulches. Their utter desolateness is an inspiration to the long, long thoughts and to the nameless wanting. Every day I walk over the sand and barrenness.

And so, then, my daily life seems an ordinary life enough, and possibly, to an ordinary person, a comfortable life.

That's as may be.

To me it is an empty, damned weariness.

I rise in the morning; eat three meals; and walk; and work a little, read a little, write; see some uninteresting people; go to bed.

Next day, I rise in the morning; eat three meals; and walk; and work a little, read a little, write; see some uninteresting people; go to bed.

Again I rise in the morning; eat three meals; and walk; and work a little, read a little, write; see some uninteresting people; go to bed.

Truly an exalted, soulful life!

What it does for me, how it affects me, I am now trying to portray.

I have in me the germs of intense life. If I could *live*, and if I could succeed in writing out my living, the world itself would feel the heavy intensity of it.

I have the personality, the nature, of a Napoleon, albeit a feminine translation. And therefore I do not conquer; I do not even fight. I manage only to exist.

Poor little Mary MacLane!—what might you not be? What wonderful things might you not do? But held down, half-buried, a seed fallen in barren ground, alone, uncomprehended, obscure—poor little Mary MacLane! Weep, world,—why don't you?—for poor little Mary MacLane!

Had I been born a man I would by now have made a deep impression of myself on the world—on some part of it. But I am a woman, and God, or the Devil, or Fate, or whosoever it was, has flayed me of the thick outer skin and thrown me out into the midst of life—has left me a lonely, damned thing filled with the red, red blood of ambition and desire, but afraid to be touched, for there is no thick skin between my sensitive flesh and the world's fingers.

But I want to be touched.

Napoleon was a man, and though sensitive his flesh was safely covered.

But I am a woman, awakening, and upon awakening and looking about me, I would fain turn and go back to sleep.

There is a pain that goes with these things when one is a woman, young, and all alone.

I am filled with an ambition. I wish to give to the world a naked Portrayal of Mary MacLane: her wooden heart, her good young woman's-body, her mind, her soul.

I wish to write, write, write!

I wish to acquire that beautiful, benign, gentle, satisfying thing—Fame. I want it—oh, I want it! I wish to leave all my obscurity, my misery—my weary unhappiness—behind me forever.

I am deadly, deadly tired of my unhappiness.

I wish this Portrayal to be published and launched into that deep salt sea—the world. There are some there surely who will understand it and me.

Can I be that thing which I am—can I be possessed of a peculiar rare genius, and yet drag out my life in obscurity in this uncouth, warped, Montana town?

It must be impossible! If I thought the world contained nothing more than that for me—oh, what should I do? Would I make an end of my dreary little life now? I fear I would. I am a philosopher—and a coward. And it were infinitely better to die now in the high-beating pulses of youth than to drag on, year after year, year after year, and find oneself at last a stagnant old woman, spiritless, hopeless, with a declining body, a declining mind,—and nothing to look back upon except the visions of things that might have been—and the weariness.

I see the picture. I see it plainly. Oh, kind Devil, deliver me from it!

Surely there must be in a world of manifold beautiful things something among them for me. And always, while I am still young, there is that dim light, the Future. But it is indeed a dim, dim light, and ofttimes there's a treachery in it.

S O THEN, yes. I find myself at this stage of womankind and nineteen years, a genius, a thief, a liar—a general moral vagabond, a fool more or less, and a philosopher of the peripatetic school. Also I find that even this combination can not make one happy. It serves, however, to occupy my versatile mind, to keep me wondering what it is a kind Devil has in store for me.

A philosopher of my own peripatetic school—hour after hour I walk over the desolate sand and dreariness among tiny hills and gulches on the outskirts of this mining town; in the morning, in the long afternoon, in the cool of the night. And hour after hour, as I walk, through my brain some long, long pageants march: the pageant of my fancies, the pageant of my unparalleled egotism, the pageant of my unhappiness, the pageant of my minute analyzing, the pageant of my peculiar philosophy, the pageant of my dull, dull life,— and the pageant of the Possibilities.

We three go out on the sand and barrenness: my wooden heart, my good young woman's-body, my soul. We go there and contemplate the long sandy wastes, the red, red line on the sky at the setting of the sun, the cold gloomy mountains under it, the ground without a weed, without a grass-blade even in their season—for they have years ago been killed of the by the sulphur smoke from the smelters.

So this sand and barrenness forms the setting for the personality of me.

I FEEL about forty years old.
Yet I know my feeling is not the feeling of forty years. These are the feelings of miserable, wretched youth.

Every day the atmosphere of a house becomes unbearable, so every day I go out to the sand and barrenness. It is not cold, neither is it mild. It is gloomy.

I sit for two hours on the ground by the side of a pitiably small narrow stream of water. It is not even a natural stream. I dare say it comes from some mine among the hills. But it is well enough that the stream is not natural—when you consider the sand and barrenness. It is singularly appropriate.

And I am singularly appropriate to all of them. It is good, after all, to be appropriate to something—to be in touch with something, even sand and barrenness. The sand and barrenness is old—oh, very old. You think of this when you look at it.

What should I do if the earth were made of wood, with a paper sky!

I feel about forty years old.

And again I say I know my feeling is not the feeling of forty years. These are the feelings of miserable, wretched youth.

Still more pitiable than the sand and barrenness and the poor unnatural stream is the dry, warped cemetery where the dry, warped people of Butte bury their dead friends. It is a source of satisfaction to me to walk down to this cemetery and contemplate it, and revel in its utter pitiableness.

"It is more pitiable than I and my sand and barrenness and my poor unnatural stream," I say over and over, and take my comfort.

Its condition is more forlorn than that of a woman young and alone. It is unkempt. It is choked with dust and stones. The few scattered blades of grass look rather ashamed to be seen growing there. A great many of the headstones are of wood and are in a shameful state of decay. Those that are of stone are still more shameful in their hard brightness.

The dry, warped friends of the dry, warped people of Butte are buried in this dusty, dreary, wind-havocked waste. They are left here and forgotten.

The Devil must rejoice in this graveyard.

And I rejoice with the Devil.

It is something for me to contemplate that is more pitiable than I and my sand and barrenness and my unnatural stream.

I rejoice with the Devil.

The inhabitants of this cemetery are forgotten. I have watched once the burying of a young child. Every day for a fortnight afterward I came back, and I saw the mother of the child there.

She came and stood by the small new grave. After a few days more she stopped coming.

I knew the woman and went to her house to see her. She was beginning to forget the child. She was beginning to take up again the thread of her life where she had let it go. The thread of her life is involved in the divorces and fights of her neighbors.

Out in the warped graveyard her child is forgotten. And presently the wooden headstone will begin to decay. But the worms will not forget their part. They have eaten the small body by now, and enjoyed it. Always worms enjoy a body to eat.

And also the Devil rejoiced.

And I rejoiced with the Devil.

They are more pitiable, I insist, than I and my sand and barrenness—the mother whose life is involved in divorces and fights, and the worms eating at the child's body, and the wooden headstone which will presently decay.

And so the Devil and I rejoice.

But no matter how ferociously pitiable is the dried-up graveyard, the sand and barrenness and the sluggish little stream have their own persistent individual damnation. The world is at least so constructed that its treasures may be damned each in a different manner and degree.

I feel about forty years old.

And I know my feeling is not the feeling of forty years. They do not feel any of these things at forty. At forty the fire has long since burned out. When I am forty I shall look back to myself and my feelings at nineteen—and I shall smile.

Or shall I indeed smile?

AS I have said, I want Fame. I want to write—to write such things as compel the admiring acclamations of the world at large; such things as are written but once in years, things subtly but distinctly different from the books written every day.

I can do this.

Let me but make a beginning, let me but strike the world in a vulnerable spot, and I can take it by storm. Let me but win my spurs, and then you will see me—of womankind and young—valiantly astride a charger riding down the world, with Fame following at the charger's heels, and the multitudes agape.

But oh, more than all this I want to be happy!

Fame is indeed benign and gentle and satisfying. But Happiness is something at once tender and brilliant beyond all things.

I want Fame more than I can tell.

But more than I want Fame I want Happiness. I have never been happy in my weary young life.

Think, oh, *think,* of being happy for a year—for a day! How brilliantly blue the sky would be; how swiftly and joyously would the green rivers run; how madly, merrily triumphant the four winds of heaven would sweep round the corners of the fair earth!

What would I not give for one day, one hour, of that charmed thing Happiness! What would I not give up?

How we eager fools tread on each other's heels, and tear each other's hair, and scratch each other's faces, in our furious gallop after Happiness! For some it is embodied in Fame, for some in Money, for some in Power, for some in Virtue—and for me in something very much like love.

None of the other fools desires Happiness as I desire it. For one single hour of Happiness I would give up at once these things: Fame, and Money, and Power, and Virtue, and Honor, and Righteousness, and Truth, and Logic, and Philosophy, and Genius. The while I would say, What a little, little price to pay for dear Happiness!

I am ready and waiting to give all that I have to the Devil in exchange for Happiness. I have been tortured so long with the dull, dull misery of Nothingness—all my nineteen years. I want to be happy—oh, I want to be happy!

The Devil has not yet come. But I know that he usually comes, and I wait him eagerly.

I am fortunate that I am not one of those who are burdened with an innate sense of virtue and honor which must come always before Happiness. They are but few who find their Happiness in their Virtue. The rest of them must be content to see it walk away.

But with me Virtue and Honor are nothing.
I long unspeakably for Happiness.
And so I await the Devil's coming.

AND meanwhile—as I wait—my mind occupies itself with its own good odd philosophy, so that even the Nothingness becomes almost endurable.

The Devil has given me some good things—for I find that the Devil owns and rules the earth and all that therein is. He has given me, among other things—my admirable young woman's-body, which I enjoy thoroughly and of which I am passionately fond.

A spasm of pleasure seizes me when I think in some acute moment of the buoyant health and vitality of this fine young body that is feminine in every fiber.

You may gaze at and admire the picture in the front of this book. It is the picture of a genius—a genius with a good strong young woman's-body,—and inside the pictured body is a liver, a MacLane liver, of admirable perfectness.

Other young women and older women and men of all ages have good bodies also, I doubt not—though the masculine body is merely flesh, it seems, flesh and bones and nothing else. But few recognize the value of their bodies; few have grasped the possibilities, the artistic graceful perfection, the poetry of human flesh in its health. Few have even sense enough indeed to keep their flesh in health, or to know what health is until they have ruined some vital organ, and so banished it forever.

I have not ruined any of my vital organs, and I appreciate what health is. I have grasped the art, the poetry of my fine feminine body.

This at the age of nineteen is a triumph for me.

Sometime in the midst of the brightness of an October I have walked for miles in the still high air under the blue of the sky. The brightness of the day and the blue of the sky and the incomparable high air have entered into my veins and flowed with my red blood. They have penetrated into every remote nerve-center and into the marrow of my bones.

At such a time this young body glows with life.

My red blood flows swiftly and joyously— in the midst of the brightness of October.

My sound, sensitive liver rest gently with its thin yellow bile in sweet content.

My calm, beautiful stomach silently sings, as I walk, a song of peace.

My lungs, saturated with mountain ozone and the perfume of the pines, expand in continuous ecstacy.

My heart beats like the music of Schumann, in easy, graceful rhythm with an undertone of power.

My strong and sensitive nerves are reeking

and swimming in sensuality like drunken little Bacchantes, gay and garlanded in mad revelling.

The entire wonderful, graceful mechanism of my woman's-body has fallen at the time—like the wonderful, graceful mechanism of my woman's-mind—under the enchanting spell of a day in October.

"It is good," I think to myself, "oh, it is good to be alive! It is wondrously good to be a woman young in the fullness of nineteen springs. It is unutterably lovely to be a healthy young animal living on this charmed earth."

After I have walked for several hours I reach a region where the sulphur smoke has not penetrated, and I sit on the ground with drawn-up knees and rest as the shadows lengthen. The shadows lengthen early in October.

Presently I lie flat on my back and stretch my lithe slimness to its utmost like a mountain lioness taking her comfort. I am intensely thankful to the Devil for my two good legs and the full use of them under a short skirt, when, as now, they carry me out beyond the pale of civilization away from tiresome dull people. There is nothing in the world that can become so maddeningly wearisome as people, people, people!

And so, Devil, accept, for my two good legs, my sincerest gratitude. I lie on the ground for some minutes and meditate idly. There is a worldful of easy indolent, beautiful sensuality in the figure of a young woman lying on the ground under a warm setting sun. A man may lie on the ground—but that is as far as it goes. A man would go to sleep, probably, like a dog or a pig. He would even snore, perhaps—under the setting sun. But then, a man has not a good young feminine body to feel with, to receive into itself the spirit of a warm sun at its setting, on a day in October,—and so let us forgive him for sleeping, and for snoring.

When I rise again to a sitting posture all the brightness has focused itself to the west. It casts a yellow glamor over the earth, a glamor not of joy, nor of pleasure, nor of happiness—but of peace.

The young poplar trees smile gently in the deathly still air. The sage brush and the tall grass take on a radiant quietness. The high hills of Montana, near and distant, appear tender and benign. All is peace—peace. I think of that beautiful old song:

"Sweet vale of Avoca! how calm could I rest
    In thy bosom of shade—."

But I am too young yet to think of peace. It is not peace that I want. Peace is for forty and fifty. I am waiting for my Experience.

I am awaiting the coming of the Devil.

And now, just before twilight, after the sun has vanished over the edge, is the red, red line on the sky.

There will be days wild and stormy, filled with rain and wind and hail; and yet nearly always at the sun's setting there will be calm— and the red line of sky.

There is nothing in the world quite like this red sky at sunset. It is Glory, Triumph, Love, Fame!

Imagine a life bereft of things, and fingers pointed at it, and eyebrows raised; tossed and bandied hither and yon; crushed, beaten, bled, rent asunder, outraged, convulsed with pain; and then, into this life while still young, the red, red line of sky!

Why did I cry out against Fate, say the line; why did I rebel against my term of anguish! I now rather rejoice at it; now in my Happiness I remember it only with deep pleasure.

Think of that wonderful, admirable, matchless man of steel, Napoleon Bonaparte. He threw himself heavily on the world, and the world has never since been the same. He hated himself, and the world, and God, and Fate, and the Devil. His hatred was his term of anguish.

Then the sun threw on the sky for him a red, red line—the red line of Triumph, Glory, Fame!

And afterward there was the blackness of Night, the blackness that is not tender, not gentle.

But black as our Night may be, nothing can take from us the memory of the red, red sky.

"Memory is possession," and so the red sky we have with us always.

Oh, Devil, Fate, World—some one, bring me my red sky! For a little brief time, and I will be satisfied. Bring it to me intensely red, intensely full, intensely alive! Short as you will, but red, red, red!

I am weary—weary, and, oh, I want my red sky! Short as it might be, its memory, its fragrance would stay with me always—always. Bring me, Devil, my red line of sky for one hour and take all, *all*—everything I possess. Let me keep my Happiness for one short hour, and take away all from me forever. I will be satisfied when Night has come and everything is gone.

Oh, I await you, Devil, in a wild frenzy of impatience!

And as I hurry back through the cool darkness of October, I feel this frenzy in every fiber of my fervid woman's body.

I COME from a long line of Scotch and Canadian MacLanes. There are a great many MacLanes, but there is usually only one real MacLane in each generation. There is but one who feels again the passionate spirit of the clans, those barbaric dwellers in the bleak, but well-beloved Highlands of Scotland.

I am the real MacLane of my generation. The real MacLane in these later centuries is always a woman. The men of the family never amount to anything worth naming—if one accepts the acme, the zenith, of pure selfishness, with a large letter "s." Life may be easy enough for the innumerable Canadian MacLanes who are not real. But it is certain to be more or less a Hill of Difficulty for the one who is. She finds herself somewhat alone. I have brothers and a sister and a mother in the same house with me—and I find myself somewhat alone. Between them and me there is no tenderness, no sympathy, no binding ties. Would it affect me in the least—do you suppose—if they should all die tomorrow? If I were not a real MacLane perhaps it would have been different, or perhaps I should not have missed these things.

How much, Devil, have I lost for the privilege of being a real MacLane?

But yes, I have also gained much.

I HAVE said that I am alone.

I am not quite, quite alone.

I have one friend—of that Friendship that is real and is inlaid with the beautiful thing Truth. And because it has the beautiful thing Truth in it, this my one Friendship is somehow above and beyond me; there is something in it that I reach after in vain—for I have not that divinely beautiful thing Truth. Have I not said that I am a thief and a liar? But in this Friendship nevertheless there is a rare, ineffably sweet something that is mine. It is the one tender thing in this dull dreariness that wraps me round.

Are there many things in this cool-hearted world so utterly exquisite as the pure love of one woman for another woman?

My one friend is a woman some twelve or thirteen years older than I. She is as different from me as is day from night. She believes in God—that God that is shown in the Bible of the Christians. And she carries with her an atmosphere of gentleness and truth. The while I am ready and waiting to dedicate my life to the Devil in exchange for Happiness—or some lesser thing. But I love Fannie Corbin with a peculiar and vivid intensity, and with all the sincerity and passion that is in me. Often I think of her, as I walk over the sand in my Nothingness, all day long. The Friendship of her and me is a fair, dear benediction upon me, but there is something in it—deep within it—that eludes me. In moments when I realize this, when I strain and reach vainly at a thing beyond me, when indeed I see in my mind a vision of the personality of Fannie Corbin, it is then that it comes on me with force that I am not good.

But I can love her with all the ardor of a young and passionate heart.

Yes, I can do that.

For a year I have loved my one friend. During the eighteen years of my life before she came into it I loved no one, for there was no one.

It is an extremely hard thing to go through eighteen years with no one to love, and no one to love you—the first eighteen years.

But now I have my one friend to love and to worship.

I have named my friend the "anemone lady," a name beautifully appropriate.

The anemone lady used to teach me literature in the Butte High School. She used to read poetry in the classroom in a clear, sweet voice that made one wish one might sit there forever and listen to it.

But now I have left the high school, and the dear anemone lady has gone from Butte. Before she went she told me she would be my friend.

Think of it—to live and have a friend!

My friend does not fully understand me; she thinks much too well of me. She has not a correct idea of my soul's depths and shallows. But if she did know them she would still be my friend. She knows the heavy weight of my unrest and unhappiness. She is tenderly sympathetic. She is the one in all the world who is dear to me.

Often I think, if only I could have my anemone lady and go and live with her in some little out-of-the-world place high up on the side of a mountain for the rest of my life—what more would I desire? My friendship would constitute my life. The unrest, the dreariness, the Nothingness of my existence now is so dull and gray by contrast that there would be Happiness for me in that life, Happiness softly radiant, if quiet—redolent of the fresh, thin fragrance of the dear blue anemone that grows in the winds and rains of spring.

But Miss Corbin would doubtless look somewhat askance at the idea of spending the rest of her life with me on a mountain. She is very fond of me, but her feeling for me is not like mine for her, which indeed is natural. And her life is made up mostly of sacrifices—doing for her fellow-creatures, giving of herself. She never would leave this.

And so, then, the mountainside and the

solitude and the friend with me are, like every good thing, but a vision.

"Thy friend is always thy friend; not to have, nor to hold, nor to love, nor to rejoice in: but to remember."

And so do I remember my one friend, the anemone lady—and think often about her with passionate love.

HAPPINESS, don't you know, is of three kinds—and all are transitory. It never stays, but it comes and goes.

There is that happiness that comes from newly-washed feet, for instance, and a pair of clean stockings on them, particularly after one has been upon a tramp into the country. Always I have identified this kind of happiness with a Maltese cat, dipping a hungry, stealthy, sensual tongue into a bowl of fresh, thick cream.

There is that still happiness that has come to me at rare times when I have been with my one friend—and which does very well for people whose feelings are moderate. They need wish for nothing beyond it. They could not appreciate anything deeper.

And there is that kind of happiness which is of the red sunset sky. There is something terrible in the thought of this indescribable mad Happiness. What a thing it is for a human being to be *happy*—with the red, red Happiness of the sunset sky!

It's like a terrific storm in summer with rain and wind, beating quiet water into wild waves, bending great trees to the ground,—convulsing the green earth with delicious pain.

It's like something of Schubert's played on the violin that stirs you within to exquisite torture.

It's like the human voice divine singing a Scotch ballad in a manner to drag your soul from your body.

But there are no words to tell it. It is something infinitely above and beyond words. It is the kind of Happiness the Devil will bring to me when he comes, to me, to *me*! Oh, why does he not come now when I am in the midst of my youth! Why is he so long in coming?

Often you hear a dozen stories of how the Devil was most ready and willing to take all from some one and give him his measure of Happiness. And sometimes the person was innately virtuous and so could not take the Happiness when it was offered. But Happiness is its own justification, and it should be eagerly grasped when it comes.

A world filled with fools will never learn this.

And so here I stand in the midst of Nothingness waiting and longing for the Devil, and he doesn't come. I feel a choking, strangling, frenzied feeling of waiting—oh, why doesn't my Happiness come! I have waited so long—so long.

There are persons who say to me that I ought not to think of the Devil, that I ought not to think of Happiness—Happiness for me would be sure to mean something wicked (as if Happiness could ever be wicked!); that I ought to think of being good. I ought to think of God. These are persons who help to fill the world with fools. At any rate their words are unable to affect me. I can not distinguish between right and wrong in this scheme of things. It is one of the lines of reasoning in which I have gotten to the edge, the end. I have gotten to the point to which all logic finally leads. I can only say, What is wrong? What is right? What is good? What is evil? The words are merely words, with word-meanings.

Truth is Love, and Love is the only Truth, and Love is the one thing out of all that is real.

The Devil is really the only one to whom we may turn, and he exacts payment in full for every favor.

But surely he will come one day with Happiness for me.

Yet, oh, how can I wait!

To be a woman, young and all alone, is hard—*hard*!—is to want things, is to carry a heavy, heavy weight.

Oh, damn! damn! damn! Damn every living thing, the world!—the universe be damned!

Oh, I am weary, weary! Can't you see that I am weary and pity me in my own damnation?

IT IS night. I might well be in my bed taking a needed rest. But first I shall write.

To-day I walked far away over the sand in the teeth of a bitter wind. The wind was determined that I should turn and come back, and equally I was determined I would go on. I went on.

There is a certain kind of wind in the autumn to walk in the midst of which causes one's spirits to rise ecstatically. To walk in the midst of a bitter wind in January may have almost any effect.

To-day the bitter wind swept over me and around me and into the remote corners of my brain and swept away the delusions, and buffeted my philosophy with rough insolence.

The world is made up mostly of nothing. You may be convinced of this when a bitter wind has swept away your delusions.

What is the wind?

Nothing.

What is the sky?

Nothing.

What do we know?

Nothing.

What is fame?

Nothing.

What is my heart?

Nothing.

What is my soul?

Nothing.

What are we?

We are nothing.

We think we progress wonderfully in the arts and sciences as one century follows another. What does it amount to? It does not teach us the all-why. It does not let us cease to wonder what it is that we are doing, where it is that we are going. It does not teach us why the green comes again to the old, old hills in the spring; why the benign balm-o'-Gilead shines wet and sweet after the rain; why the red never fails to come to the breast of the robin, the black to the crow, the gray to the little wren; why the sand and barrenness lies stretched out around us; why the clouds float high above us; why the moon stands in the sky, night after night; why the mountains and valleys live on as the years pass.

The arts and sciences go on and on—still we wonder. We have not yet ceased to weep. And we suffer still in 1902, even as they suffered in 1802, and in 802.

To-day we eat our good dinners with forks.

A thousand years ago they had no forks.

Yet, though we have forks, we are not happy. We scream and kick and struggle and weep just as they did a thousand years ago—when they had no forks.

We are "no wiser than when Omar fell asleep."

And in the midst of our great wondering, we wonder why some of us are given faith to trust without question, while the rest of us are left to eat out our life's vitals with asking.

I have walked once in summer by the side of a little marsh filled with mint and white hawthorn. The mint and white hawthorn have with them a vivid, rare, delicious perfume. It makes you want to grovel on the ground—it makes you think you might crawl in the dust all your days, and well for you. The perfume lingers with you afterward when years have passed. You may scream and kick and struggle and weep right lustily every day of your life, but in your moments of calmness sometimes there will come back to you the fragrance of a swamp filled with mint and white hawthorn.

It is meltingly beautiful.

What does it mean?

What would it tell?

Why does the marsh, and the mint and white hawthorn, freeze over in the fall? And why do they come again, voluptuous, enticing, in the damp spring days—and rack the souls of wretches who look and wonder?

You are superb, Devil! You have done a magnificent piece of work. I kneel at your feet and worship you. You have wrought a perfection, a pinnacle of fine, invisible damnation.

The world is like a little marsh filled with mint and white hawthorn. It is filled with things likewise damnably beautiful. There are the green, green grass-blades and the gray dawns; there are swiftly-flowing rivers and the honking of wild geese, flying low; there are human voices and human eyes; there are stories of women and men who have learned to give up and to wait; there is poetry; there is Charity; there is Truth.

The Devil has made all of these things, and also he has made human beings who can feel.

Who was it that said, long ago, "Life is always a tragedy to those who feel"?

In truth, the Devil has constructed a place of infinite torture—the fair green earth, the world.

But he has made that other infinite thing—Happiness. I forgive him for making me wonder, since possibly he may bring me Happiness. I cast myself at his feet. I adore him.

The first third of our lives is spent in the expectation of Happiness. Then it comes, perhaps, and stays ten years, or a month, or three days, and the rest of our lives is spent in peace and rest—with the memory of the Happiness.

Happiness—though it is infinite—is a transient emotion.

It is too brilliant, too magnificent, too overwhelming to be a lasting thing. And it is merely an emotion. But, ah—*such* an emotion!

Through it the Devil rules his domains. What would one not do to have it!

I can think of no so-called vile deed that I would scruple about if I could be happy. Everything is justified if it gives me Happiness. The Devil has done me some great favors; he has made me without a conscience, and without Virtue.

For which I thank thee, Devil.

At least I shall be able to take my Happiness when it comes—even though the piles of nice distinctions between it and me be mountains high.

But meanwhile, the world, I say, and the people are nothing, nothing, nothing. The splendid castles, the strong bridges, that we are building are of small moment. We can only go down the wide roadway wondering and weeping, and without where to lay our heads.

I HAVE eaten my dinner.

I have had, among other things, fine, rare-broiled porterhouse steak from Omaha, and some fresh, green young onions from California. And just now I am a philosopher, pure and simple—except that there's nothing very pure about my philosophy, nor yet very simple.

Let the Devil come and go; let the wild waters rush over me; let nations rise and fall; let my favorite theories form themselves in line suddenly and run into the ground; let the little earth be bandied about from one belief to another; but, I say in the midst of my young peripatetic philosophy, I need not be in complete despair—the world still contains things for me, while I have my fine rare porterhouse steak from Omaha—and my fresh green young onions from California.

Fame may pass over my head; money may escape me; my one friend may fail me; every hope may fold its tent and steal away; Happiness may remain a sealed book; every remnant of human ties may vanish; I may find myself an outcast; good things held out to me may suddenly be withdrawn; the stars may go out, one by one; the sun may go dark; yet still I may hold upright my head, if I have but my steak—and my onions.

I may find myself crowded out from many

charmed circles; I may find the ethical world too small to contain me; the social world may also exclude me; the professional world may know me not; likewise the worlds of the arts and the sciences; I may find myself superfluous in literary haunts; I may see myself going gladly back to the vile dust from whence I sprung—to live in a green forest like the melancholy Jacques; but fare they well, I will say with what cheerfulness I can summon, while I have my steak—and my onions.

Possibly I may grow old and decrepit; my hair may turn gray; my bones may become rheumatic; I may grow weak in the knees; my ankle-joints which have withstood many a peripatetic journey may develop dropsical tendencies; my heart may miss a beat now and then; my lungs may begin to fight shy of wintry blasts; my eyes may fail me; my figure that is now in its slim gracefulness may swathe itself in layers of flesh, or worse, it may wither and decay and stoop at the shoulders; my red blood may flow sluggishly; but if I still have left teeth to eat with, why need I lament while I have my steak—and my onions?

I am obscure; I am morbid; I am unhappy; my life is made up of Nothingness; I want everything and I have nothing; I have been made to feel the "lure of green things growing," and I have been made to feel also that something of them is withheld from me; I have felt the deadly tiredness that is among the birthrights of a human being; but with it all the Devil has given me a philosophy of my own—the Devil has enabled me to count, if need be, the world well lost for a fine rare porterhouse steak—and some green young onions.

For which I thank thee, Devil, profoundly.

Who says the Devil is not your friend? Who says the Devil does not believe in the all-merciful Law of Compensation?

And so it is—do you see?—that all things look different after a satisfying dinner, that the color of the world changes, that life in fact resolves itself into two things: a fine rare-broiled porterhouse steak from Omaha, and some fresh green young onions from California.

I AM charmingly original. I am delightfully refreshing. I am startlingly Bohemian. I am quaintly interesting—the while in my sleeve I may be smiling and smiling—and a villain. I can talk to a roomful of dull people and compel their interest, admiration, and astonishment. I do this sometimes for my own amusement. As I have said, I am a rather plain-featured, insignificant-looking genius, but I have a graceful personality. I have a pretty figure. I am well set up. And when I choose to talk in my charmingly original fashion, embellishing my conversation with many quaint lies, I have a certain very noticeable way with me, an "air."

It is well, if one has nothing else, to acquire an air. And an air taken in conjunction with my charming originality, my delightfully refreshing candor, is something powerful and striking in its way.

I do not, however, exert myself often in this way; partly because I can sometimes foresee, from the character of the assembled company, that my performance will not have the desired effect—for I am a genius, and genius at close range at times carries itself unconsciously to the point where it becomes so interesting that it is atrocious, and can not be carried farther without having somewhat mildly disastrous results; and then, again, the facial antics of some ten or a dozen persons possessed more or less of the qualities of the genus fool—even they become tiresome after a while.

Always I talk about myself on an occasion of this kind. Indeed, my conversation is on all occasions devoted directly or indirectly to myself.

When I talk on the subject of ethics, I talk of it as it is related to Mary MacLane.

When I give out broad-minded opinions about Ninon de l'Enclos, I demonstrate her relative position to Mary MacLane!

When I discourse liberally on the subject of the married relation, I talk of it only as it will affect Mary MacLane.

An interesting creature, Mary MacLane.

As a matter of fact, it is so with every one, only every one is far from realizing and acknowledging it. And I have not lacked listeners, though these people do not appreciate me. They do not realize that I am a genius.

I am of womankind and of nineteen years. I am able to stand off and gaze critically and dispassionately at myself and my relation to my environment, to the world, to everything the world contains. I am able to judge whether I am good and whether I am bad. I am able, indeed, to tell what I am and where I stand. I can see far, far inward. I am a genius,

Charlotte Bronte did this in some degree, and she was a genius; and also Marie

Bashkirtseff, and Olive Schreiner, and George Eliot. They are all geniuses.

And so, then, I am a genius—a genius in my own right.

I am fundamentally, organically egotistic. My vanity and self-conceit have attained truly remarkable development as I've walked and walked in the loneliness of the sand and barrenness. Not the least remarkable part of it is that I know my egotism and vanity thoroughly—thoroughly, and plume myself thereon.

These are the ear-marks of a genius—and of a fool. There is a finely-drawn line between a genius and a fool. Often this line is overstepped and your fool becomes a genius, or your genius becomes a fool.

It is but a tiny step.

There's but a tiny step between the great and the little, the tender and the contemptuous, the sublime and the ridiculous, the aggressive and the humble, the paradise and the perdition.

And so is it between the genius and the fool.

I am a genius.

I am not prepared to say how many times I may overstep the finely-drawn line, or how many times I have already overstepped it. 'Tis a matter of small moment.

I have entered into certain things marvelously deep. I know things, I know that I know them, and I know that I know that I know them, which is a fine psychological point.

It is magnificent of me to have gotten so far, at the age of nineteen, with no training other than that of the sand and barrenness. Magnificent—do you hear?

Very often I take this fact in my hand and squeeze it hard like an orange, to get the sweet, sweet juice from it. I squeeze a great deal of juice from it every day, and every day the juice is renewed, like the vitals of Prometheus. And so I squeeze and squeeze, and drink the juice, and try to be satisfied.

Yes, you may gaze long and curiously at the portrait in the front of this book. It is of one who is a genius of egotism and analysis, a genius who is awaiting the Devil's coming,—a genius, with a wondrous liver within.

I shall tell you more about this liver, I think, before I have done.

I CAN remember a time long, oh, very long ago. That is the time when I was a child. It is ten or a dozen years ago.

Or is it a thousand years ago?

It is when you have but just parted from your friend that he seems farthest from you. When I have lived several more years the time when I was a child will not seem so far behind me.

Just now it is frightfully far away. It is so far away that I can see it plainly outlined on the horizon.

It is there always for me to look at. And when I look I can feel the tears deep within me—a salt ocean of tears that roll and surge and swell bitterly in a dull, mad anguish, and never come to the surface.

I do not know which is the more weirdly and damnably pathetic: I when I was a child, or I when I am grown to a woman, young and all alone. I weigh the question coldly and logically, but my logic trembles with rage and grief and unhappiness.

When I was a child I lived in Canada and in Minnesota. I was a little wild savage. In Minnesota there were swamps where I used to wet my feet in the spring, and there were fields of tall grass where I would lie flat on my stomach in company with lizards and little garter snakes.

And there were poplar leaves that turned their pale green backs upward on a hot afternoon, and soon there would be terrific thunder and lightning and rain. And there were robins that sang at dawn. These things stay with one always. And there were children with whom I used to play and fight.

I was tanned and sunburned, and I had an unkempt appearance. My face was very dirty. The original pattern of my frock was invariable lost in layers and vistas of the native soil. My hair was braided or else it flew about, a tangled maze, according as I could be caught by some one and rubbed and straightened before I ran away for the day. My hands were little and strong and brown, and wrought much mischief. I came and went at my own pleasure. I ate what I pleased; I went to bed all in my own good time; I tramped wherever my stubborn little feet chose. I was impudent; I was contrary; I had an extremely bad temper; I was hard-hearted; I was full of infantile malice. Truly I was a vicious little beast.

I was a little piece of untrained Nature.

And I am unable to judge which is the more savagely forlorn: the starved-hearted child, or the woman, young and all alone.

The little wild stubborn child felt things and wanted things. She did not know that she felt things and wanted things.

Now I feel and I want things and I know it with burning vividness.

The little vicious Mary MacLane suffered, but she did not know that she suffered. Yet that did not make the suffering less.

And she reached out with a little sunburned hand to touch and take something.

But the sunburned little hand remained empty. There was nothing for it. No one had anything to put into it.

The little wild creature wanted to be loved; she wanted something to put in her hungry little heart.

But no one had anything to put into a hungry little heart.

No one said "dear."

The little vicious child was the only MacLane, and she felt somewhat alone. But there, after all, were the lizards and the little garter snakes.

The wretched, hardened little piece of untrained Nature has grown and developed into a woman, young and alone.

For the child there was a Nothingness, and for the woman there is a great Nothingness.

Perhaps the Devil will bring me something in my lonely womanhood to put in my wooden heart.

But the time when I was a child will never come again. It is gone—gone. I may live through some long, long years, but nothing like it will ever come. For there is nothing like it.

It is a life by itself. It has naught to do with philosophy, or with genius, or with heights and depths, or with the red sunset sky, or with the Devil.

These come later.

The time of the child is a thing apart. It is the Planting and Seed time. It is the Beginning of things. It decides whether there shall be brightness or bitterness in the long after years.

I have left that time far enough behind me. It will never come back. And it had a Nothingness—do you hear, a *Nothingness!* Oh, the pity of it! the pity of it!

Do you know why it is that I look back to the horizon at the figure of an unkempt, rough child, and why I feel a surging torrent of tears and anguish and despair?

I feel more than that indeed, but I have no words to tell it.

I shall have to miss forever some beautiful, wonderful things because of that wretched, lonely childhood.

There will always be a lacking, a wanting— some dead branches that never grew leaves.

It is not deaths and murders and plots and wars that make life tragedy.

It is Nothing that makes life tragedy.

It is day after day, and year after year, and Nothing.

It is a sunburned little hand reached out and Nothing put into it.

I SIT at my window and look out upon the housetops and chimneys of Butte. As I look I have a weary, disgusted feeling.

People are abominable creatures.

Under each of the roofs live a man and woman joined together by that very slender thread, the marriage ceremony—and their children, the result of the marriage ceremony.

How many of them love each other? Not two in a hundred, I warrant. The marriage ceremony is their one miserable, petty, paltry excuse for living together.

This marriage rite, it appears, is often used as a cloak to cover a world of rather shameful things.

How virtuous these people are, to be sure, under their different roof-trees. So virtuous are they indeed that they are able to draw themselves up in the pride of their own purity, when they happen upon some corner where the marriage ceremony is lacking. So virtuous are they that the men can afford to find amusement and diversion in the woes of the corner that is without the marriage rite; and the women may draw away their skirts in shocked horror and wonder that such things can be, in view of their own spotless virtue.

And so they live on under the roofs, and they eat and work and sleep and die; and the children grow up and seek other roofs, and call upon the marriage ceremony even as their parents before them—and then they likewise eat and work and sleep and die; and so on world without end.

This also is life—the life of the good, virtuous Christians.

I think, therefore, that I should prefer some life that is not virtuous.

I shall never make use of the marriage ceremony. I hereby register a vow, Devil, to that effect.

When a man and a woman love one another that is enough. That is marriage. A religious rite is superfluous. And if the man and woman live together without the love, no ceremony in the world can make it marriage. The woman who does this need not feel the tiniest bit better than her lowest sister in the streets. Is she not indeed a step lower since she pretends to be what she is not—plays the virtuous woman? While the other unfortunate pretends nothing. She wears her name on her sleeve.

If I were obliged to be one of these I would rather be she who wears her name on her sleeve. I certainly would. The lesser of two evils, always.

I can think of nothing in the world like the utter littleness, the paltriness, the contemptibleness, the degradation, of the woman who is tied down under a roof with a man who is really nothing to her; who wears the man's name, who bears the man's children—who plays the virtuous woman. There are too many such in the world now.

May I never, I say, become that abnormal, merciless animal, that deformed monstrosity—a virtuous woman.

Anything, Devil, but that.

And so, as I look out over the roofs and chimneys, I have a weary, disgusted feeling.

THIS is not a diary. It is a Portrayal. It is my inner life shown in its nakedness. I am trying my utmost to show everything—to reveal every petty vanity and weakness, every phase of feeling, every desire. It is a remarkably hard thing to do, I find, to probe my soul to its depths, to expose its shades and half-lights.

Not that I am troubled with modesty or shame. Why should one be ashamed of anything?

But there are elements in one's mental equipment so vague, so opaque, so undefined— how is one to grasp them? I have analyzed and analyzed, and I have gotten down to some extremely fine points—yet still there are things upon my own horizon that go beyond me.

There are feelings that rise and rush over me overwhelmingly. I am helpless, crushed, and defeated before them. It is as if they were written on the walls of my soul-chamber in an unknown language.

My soul goes blindly seeking, seeking, asking. Nothing answers. I cry out after some unknown Thing with all the strength of my being; every nerve and fiber in my young woman's-body and my young woman's-soul reaches and strains in anguished unrest. At times as I hurry over my sand and barrenness all my life's manifold passions culminate in utter rage and woe. Waves of intense, hopeless longing rush over me and envelop me round and round. My heart, my soul, my mind go wandering— wandering; ploughing their way through darkness with never a ray of light; groping with helpless hands; asking, longing, wanting things: pursued by a Demon of Unrest.

I shall go mad—I shall go mad, I say over and over to myself.

But no. No one goes mad. The Devil does not propose to release any one from a so beautifully-wrought, artistic damnation. He looks to it that one's senses are kept fully intact, and he fastens to them with steel chains the Demon of Unrest.

It hurts—oh, it tortures me in the days and days! But when the Devil brings me my Happiness I will forgive him all this.

When my Happiness is given me, the Unrest will still be with me, I doubt not, but the Happiness will change the tenor of it, will make it an instrument of joy, will clasp hands with it and mingle itself with it,—the while I, with my wooden heart, my woman's-body, my mind, my soul, shall be in transports. I shall be filled with pleasure so deep and pain so intense that my being's minutest nerve will reel and stagger in intoxication, will go drunk with the fullness of Life.

When my Happiness is given me I shall live centuries in the hours. And we shall all grow old rapidly,—I and my wooden heart, and my woman's-body, and my mind, and my soul. Sorrow may age one in some degree. But Happiness—the real Happiness—rolls countless years off from one's fingertips in a single moment, and each year leaves its impress.

It is true that life is a tragedy to those who feel. When my Happiness is given me life will be an ineffable, a nameless thing.

It will seethe and roar; it will plunge and whirl; it will leap and shriek in convulsion; it will guiver in delicate fantasy; it will writhe and twist; it will glitter and flash and shine; it will sing gently; it will shout in exquisite excitement; it will vibrate to the roots like a great oak in a storm; it will dance; it will glide; it will gallop; it will rush; it will swell and surge; it will fly; it will soar high—high; it will go down into depths unexplored; it will rage and rave; it will yell in utter joy; it will melt; it will blaze; it will ride triumphant; it will grovel in the dust of entire pleasure; it will sound out like a terrific blare of trumpets; it will chime faintly, faintly like the remote tinkling notes of a harp; it will sob and grieve and weep; it will revel and carouse; it will shrink; it will go in pride; it will lie prone like the dead; it will float buoyantly on air; it will moan, shiver, burst—oh, it will reek with Love and Light!

The words of the English language are futile. There are no words in it, or in any other, to express an idea of that thing which would be my life in its Happiness.

The words I have written describe it, it is true,—but confusedly and inadequately.

But words are for everyday use.

When it comes my turn to meet face to face the unspeakable vision of the Happy Life I shall be rendered dumb.

But the rains of my feeling will come in torrents!

I AM an artist of the most artistic, the highest type. I have uncovered for myself the art that lies in obscure shadows. I have discovered the art of the day of small things.

And that surely is art with a capital "A."

I have acquired the art of Good Eating. Usually it is in the gray and elderly forties and fifties that people cultivate this art—if they ever do; it is indeed a rare art.

But I know it in all its rare exquisiteness at the young slim age of nineteen—which is one more mark of my genius, do you see?

The art of Good Eating has two essential points: one must eat only when one is hungry, and one must take small bites.

There are persons who eat for the sake of eating. They are gourmands, and partake of the natures of the pig and the buzzard. There are persons who take bites that are not small. These also are gourmands and partake of the natures of the pig and the buzzard. There are persons who can enjoy nothing in the way of eating except a luxurious, well-appointed meal. These, it is safe to say, have not acquired the art of anything.

But I—I have acquired the art of eating an olive.

Now listen, and I will tell you the art of eating an olive:

I take the olive in my fingers, and I contemplate its green oval richness. It make me think at once of the land where the green citron grows—where the cypress and myrtle are emblems; of the land of the Sun where human beings are delightfully, enchantingly wicked,—where the men are eager and passionate, and the women gracefully developed in mind and in body—and their two breasts show round and full and delicately veined beneath thin drapery.

The mere sight of the olive conjures up this charming picture in my mind.

I set my teeth and my tongue upon the olive, and bite it. It is bitter, salt, delicious. The saliva rushes to meet it, and my tongue is a happy tongue. As the morsel of olive rests in my mouth and is crunched and squeezed lusciously among my teeth, a quick, temporary change takes place in my character. I think of some adorable lines of the Persian poet: "Give thyself up to joy, for thy Grief will be infinite. The stars shall again meet together at the same point in the firmament, but of thy body shall bricks be made for a palace wall."

"Oh, dear, sweet, bitter olive!" I say to myself.

The bit of olive slips down my red gullet, and so into my stomach. There it meets with a joyous welcome. Gastric juices leap out from the walls and swathe it in loving embrace. My stomach is fond of something bitter and salt. It lavishes flattery and endearment galore upon the olive. It laughs in silent delight. It feels that the day it has long waited for has come. The philosophy of my stomach is wholly epicurean. Let it receive but a tiny bit of olive and it will reck not of the morrow, nor of the past. It lives, voluptuously, in the present. It is content. It is in paradise.

I bite the olive again. Again the bitter salt crisp ravishes my tongue. "If this be vanity, vanity let it be." The golden moments flit by and I heed them not. For am I not comfortably seated and eating an olive? Go hang yourself, you who have never been comfortably seated and eating an olive! My character evolves farther in its change. I am now bent on reckless sensuality, let happen what will. The fair earth seems to resolve itself into a thing oval and crisp and good and green and deliciously salt. I experience a feeling of fervent gladness that I am a female thing living, and that I have a tongue and some teeth, and salivary glands.

Also this bit slips down my red gullet, and again the festive Stomach lifts up a silent voice in psalms and rejoicing. It is now an absolute monarchy with the green olive at its head. The kisses of the gastric juice become hot and sensual and convulsive and ecstatic. "Avaunt, pale, shadowy ghosts of dyspepsia!" says my

Stomach. "I know you not. I am of a brilliant, shining world. I dwell in Elysian fields."

Once more I bite the olive. Once more is my tongue electrified. And the third stage in my temporary transformation takes place. I am now a gross but supremely contented sensualist. An exquisite symphony of sensualism and pleasure seems to play somewhere within me. My heart purrs. My brain folds its arms and lounges. I put my feet up on the seat of another chair. The entire world is now surely one delicious green olive. My mind is capable of conceiving but one idea—that of a green olive. Therefore the green olive is a perfect thing—absolutely a perfect thing.

Disgust and disapproval are excited only by imperfections. When a thing is perfect, no matter how hard one may look at it, one can see only itself—and nothing beyond.

And so I have made my olive and my art perfect.

Well, then, this third bit of olive slides down the willing gullet into my stomach. "And then my heart with pleasure fills." The play of the gastric secretions is now marvelous. It is the meeting of the waters! It were well, ah, how well, if the hearts of the world could mingle in peace, as the gastric juices mingle at the coming of a green olive into my stomach! "Paradise! Paradise!" says my Stomach.

Every drop of blood in my passionate veins is resting. Through my stomach—my *stomach*, do you hear—my soul seems to feel the infinite. The minutes are flying. Shortly it will be over. But just now I am safe. I am entirely satisfied. I want nothing, nothing.

My inner quiet is infinite. I am conscious that it is but momentary, and it matters not. On the contrary, the knowledge of this fact renders the present quiet—the repose, more limitless, more intense.

Where now, Devil, is your damnation? If this be damnation, damnation let it be! If this be the human fall, then how good it is to be fallen! At this moment I would fain my fall were like yours, Lucifer, "never to hope again."

And so, bite by bite, the olive enters into my body and soul. Each bite brings with it a recurring wave of sensation and charm.

No. We will not dispute with the brilliant mind that declared life a tragedy to those who feel. We will let that stand. However, there are parts of the tragedy that are not tragic. There are parts that admit of a turning aside.

As the years pass, one after another, I shall continue to eat. And as I eat I shall have my quiet, my brief period of aberration.

This is the art of Eating.

I have acquired it by means of self-examination, analyzing—analyzing—analyzing.

Truly my genius is analytical. And it enables me to endure—if also to feel bitterly—the heavy, heavy weight of life.

What a worm of misery I should be were it not for these bursts of philosophy, these turnings aside!

If it please the Devil, one day I may have Happiness. That will be all-sufficient. I shall then analyze no more. I shall be a different being.

But meanwhile I shall eat.

When the last of the olive vanishes into the stomach, when it is there reduced to animated chyme, when I play with the olive-seed in my fingers, when I lean back in my chair and straighten out my spinal column,—oh, then do you not envy me, you fine, brave world, who are not a philosopher, who have not discovered the art of the small things, who have not conscious chyme in your stomach, who have not acquired the art of Good Eating!

A S I read over now and then what I have written of my Portrayal I have alternate periods of hope and despair. At times I think I am succeeding admirably—and again, what I have written compared to what I have felt seems vapid and tame. Who has not felt the futility of words when one would express feelings?

I take this hope and despair as another mark of genius. Genius, apart from natural sensitiveness, is prone equally to unreasoning joy and to bitterest morbidness.

I am more than fond of writing, though I have hours when I can not write any more than I could paint a picture, or play Wagner as it should be played.

I think my style of writing has a wonderful intensity in it, and it is admirably suited to the creature it portrays. What sort of Portrayal of myself would I produce if I wrote with the long, elaborate periods of Henry James, or with the pleasant, ladylike phrasing of Howells? It would be rather like a little tin phonograph trolling out flowery poetry at breakneck speed, or like a deep-toned church organ pouring forth "Goo-Goo Eyes" with ponderous feeling.

When I read a book I study it carefully to find whether the author *knows things,* and whether I could, with the same subject, write a better one myself.

The latter question I usually decide in the affirmative.

The highest thing one can do in literature is to succeed in saying that thing which one meant to say. There is nothing better than that—to make the world see your thoughts as you see them. Eugene Field and Edgar Allan Poe and Robert Louis Stevenson and Charles Dickens, among others, have succeeded in doing this. They impress the world with a sense of their courage and realness.

There are people who have written books which did not impress the world in this way, but which nevertheless came out of the feeling and fullness of zealous hearts. Always I think of that pathetic, artless little old-fashioned thing, "Jane Eyre," as a picture shown to a world seeing with distorted vision. Charlotte Bronté meant one thing when she wrote the book, and the world after a time suddenly understood a quite different thing, and heaped praise and applause upon her therefor. When I read the book I was not quite able to see just what the message was that the Bronté intended to send out. But I saw that there was a message— of bravery, perhaps, or of that good which may come out of Nazareth. But the world that praised and applauded and gave her money seems totally to have missed it.

It takes centuries of tears and piety and mourning to move this world a tiny bit.

But still it will give you praise and applause and money if you will prostitute your sensibilities and emotions for the gratification of it.

I have no message to hide in a book and send out. I am writing a Portrayal.

But a Portrayal is also a thing that may be misunderstood.

AN IDLE brain is the Devil's workshop, they say. It is an absurdly incongruous statement. If the Devil is at work in a brain it certainly is not idle. And when one considers how brilliant a personage the Devil is, and what very fine work he turns out, it becomes an open question whether he would have the slightest use for most of the idle brains that cumber the earth. But, after all, the Devil is so clever that he could produce unexcelled workmanship with even the poorest tools.

My brain is one kind of devil's workshop, and it is as incessantly hard-worked and always-busy a one as you could imagine.

It is a devil's workshop, indeed, only I do the work myself. But there is a mental telegraphy between the Devil and me, which accounts for the fact that many of my ideas are so wonderfully groomed and perfumed and colored. I take no credit to myself for this, though, as I say, I do the work myself.

I try always to give the Devil his due—and particularly in this Portrayal.

There are very few who give the Devil his due in this world of hypocrites.

I never think of the Devil as that atrocious creature in red tights, with cloven hoofs and a tail and a two-tined fork. I think of him rather as an extremely fascinating, strong, steel-willed person in conventional clothes—a man with whom to fall completely, madly in love. I rather think, I believe, that he is incarnate at times. Why not?

Periodically I fall completely, madly in love with the Devil. He is so fascinating, so strong— so strong, exactly the sort of man whom my wooden heart awaits. I would like to throw myself at his head. I would make him a dear little wife. He would love me—he would love me. I would be in raptures. And I would love him, oh, madly, madly!

"What would you have me do, little MacLane?" the Devil would say.

"I would have you conquer me, crush me, know me," I would answer.

"What shall I say to you?" the Devil would ask.

"Say to me, 'I love you, I love you, I love you,' in your strong, steel, fascinating voice. Say it to me often, always—a million times."

"What would you have me do, little MacLane?" he would say again.

I would answer: "Hurt me, burn me, consume me with hot love, shake me violently, embrace me hard, *hard* in your strong, steel arms, kiss me with wonderful burning kisses— press your lips to mine with passion, and your soul and mine would meet then in an anguish of joy for me!"

"How shall I treat you, little MacLane?"

"Treat me cruelly, brutally."

"How long shall I stay with you?"

"Through the life everlasting—it will be as one day; or for one day—it will be as the life everlasting."

"And what kind of children will you bear me, little MacLane?"

"I will bear wonderful, beautiful children— with great pain."

"But you hate pain," the Devil will say, "and when you are in your pain you will hate me."

"But no," I will answer, "pain that comes of you whom I love will be ineffable exaltation."

"And how will you treat me, little MacLane?"

"I will cast myself at your feet; or I will minister to you with divine tenderness; or I will charm you with fantastic deviltry; when you weep, I will melt into tears; when you rejoice, I will go wild with delight; when you go deaf I will stop my ears; when you go blind I will put out my eyes; when you go lame I will cut off my legs. Oh, I will be divinely dear, unutterably sweet!"

"Indeed you are rarely sweet," the Devil will say. And I will be in transports.

Oh, Devil, Devil, Devil!

Oh, misery, *misery* of Nothingness!

The days are long—long and very weary as I await the Devil's coming.

TO-DAY as I walked out I was impressed deeply with the wonderful beautifulness of Nature even in her barrenness. The far-distant mountains had that high, pure, transparent look, and the nearer ones were transformed completely with a wistful, beseeching attitude that reminded me of my life. It was late in the afternoon. As the sun lowered, the pure lavender of the far-away hills was tinted with faint-rose, and the gray of the nearer ones with sun-color. And the sand—my sand and barrenness—almost flushed consciously in its wide, mysterious magnitude. In the sky there was a white cloud. The sky was blue—blue almost as when I was a child. The air was very gentle. The earth seemed softened. There was an indefinite, caressing something over all that went into my soul and stirred it, and hurt it. There was that in the air which is there when something is going to happen. Only nothing ever happens. It is rare, I thought, that my sand and barrenness looks like this. I crouched on the ground, and the wondrous calm and beauty of the natural things awed and moved me with strange, still emotions.

I felt, and gazed about me, and felt again. And everything was very still. Presently my eyes filled quietly with tears.

I bent my head into the breast of a great gray rock. Oh, my soul, my soul, I said over and over, not with passion. It is so divine—the earth is so beautiful, so untainted—and I, what am I? It was so beautiful that now as I write, and it comes over me again, I can not restrain the tears.

Tears are not common.

I felt my wooden heart, my soul, quivering and sobbing with their unknown wanting. This is my soul's awakening. Ah, the pain of my soul's awakening! Is there nothing, *nothing* to help this pain? I am so lonely, so lonely—Fannie Corbin, my one friend, my dearly-loved anemone lady, I want you so much—why aren't you here! I want to feel your hand with mine as I felt it sometimes before you went away. You are the only one among a worldful of people to care a little—and I love you with all the strength and worship I can give to the things that are beautiful and true. You are the only one, the only one— and my soul is full of pain, and I am sitting alone on the ground, and my head lies on a rock's breast.—

Strange, sweet passions stirred and waked somewhere deep within me as I sat shivering on the ground. And I felt them singing far away, as if their faint voices came out of that limitless deep, deep blue above me; and it was like a choir of spirit-voices, and they sang of love and of light and of dear tender dreams, and of my soul's awakening. Why is this—and what is it that is hurting so? Is it because I am young, or is it because I am alone, or because I am a woman?

Oh, it is a hard and bitter thing to be a woman! And why—why? Is woman so foul a creature that she must need be purged by this infinite pain?

The choir of faint, sweet voices comes to me incessantly out of the blue. My wooden heart and my soul are listening to them intently. The voices are trying hard to tell me, to help me, but I can not understand. I know only that it is about pure, exalted things, and about the all-abiding love that is somewhere; and it is about the earth-love, and about Truth,—but I can not understand. And the voices sing of me the child—a song of the unloved, starved little being; and a song of the unloved, half-grown creature; and a song of me, a woman and all alone—awaiting the Devil's coming.

Oh, my soul—my soul!

A female snake is born out of its mother's white egg, and lives awhile in content among weeds and grass, and dies.

A female dog lives some years, and has bones thrown at her, and sometimes she receives a kick or a blow, and a dog-house to sleep in, and dies.

A female bird has a nest, and worms to eat, and goes south in the winter, and presently she dies.

A female toad has a swamp or a garden, some bugs and flies, contentment and then she dies.

And each of these has a male thing with her for a time, and soon there are little snakes or little dogs for her to love as much as it is given her to love—she can do no more.

And they are fortunate with their little snakes and little dogs.

A female human being is born out of her mother's fair body, branded with a strange, plague-tainted name, and let go; and lives awhile, and dies. But before she dies she awakes. There is a pain that goes with it.

And the male thing that is with her for a time is unlike a snake or a dog. It is more like a man, and there is another pain for this.

And when a little human being comes with a soul of its own there must be another awakening, for she has then reached the best and highest state that any human being can reach, though she is a female human being, and plague-tainted. And here also there is heavy soul-pain.

The name—the plague-tainted name branded upon her—means woman.

I lifted my head from the breast of the gray rock. The tears had been falling, falling. Tears are so strange! Tears from the dried-up fountain of nineteen years are like drops of water wrung out of stone. Suddenly I got up from the ground and ran quickly over the sand for several minutes. I did not dare look again at the hilltops and the deep blue, nor listen again to the voices.

Oh, with it all, I am a coward! I shrink and cringe before the pain of the dazzling lights. Yet I am waiting—longing for the most dazzling light of all: the coming of the Devil.

OH, THE wretched bitter loneliness of me!
In all the deep darkness, and the silence, there is never a faint human light, never a voice! How can I bear it—how can I bear it!

I HAVE been looking over the confessions of the Bashkirtseff. They are indeed rather like my Portrayal, but they are not so interesting, nor so intense. I have a stronger individuality than Marie Bashkirtseff, though her mind was probably in a higher state of development than mine, even when she was younger than I.

Most of her emotions are vacillating and inconsistent. She worships a God one day and blasphemes him the next. She never loves her God. Any why, then, does she have a God? Why does she not abandon him altogether? He seems to be of no use to her—except as a convenient thing on which to fasten the blame for her misfortunes.—And, after all, that is something very useful indeed.—And she loves the people about her one day, and the next day she hates them.

But in her great passion—her ambition, Marie Bashkirtseff was beautifully consistent. And what terrific storms of woe and despair must have enveloped her when she knew that within a certain period she would be dead—removed from the world, and her work left undone! The time kept creeping nearer—she must have tasted the bitterness of death indeed. She was sure of success, sure that her high-strained ambition would be gratified to its last vestige—and then, to die! It was certainly hard lines for the little Bashkirtseff.

My own despair is of an opposite nature.

There is one thing in the world that is more bitter than death—and that is life.

Suppose that I learned I was to die on the twenty-seventh of June, 1903, for instance. It would give me a soft warm wave of pleasure, I think. I might be in the depths of woe at the time; my despair might be the despair of despair; my misery utterly unceasing,—and I could say, Never mind, on the twenty-seventh of June, 1903, all will be over—dull misery, rage, Nothingness, obscurity, the unknown longing, every desire of my soul, all the pain—ended inevitably, completely on the twenty-seventh of June, 1903. I might come upon a new pain, but this, my long old torture, would cease.

You may say that I might end my life on that day, that I might do so now. I certainly shall if the pain becomes greater than I can bear—for what else is there to do? But I shall be far from satisfied in doing so. What if I were to end everything now—when perhaps the Devil may be coming to me in two years' time with Happiness?

Upon dying it might be that I should go to some wondrous fair country where there would be trees and running water, and a resting-place. Well—oh, well! But I want the earthly Happiness. I am not high-minded and spiritual. I am earthly, human—sensitive, sensuous, sensual, and, ah, dear, my soul wants its earthly Happiness!

I can not bring myself to the point of suicide while there is a possibility of Happiness remaining. But if I knew that irrevocable, inevitable death awaited me on June twenty-seventh, 1903, I should be satisfied. My Happiness might come before that time, or it might not. I should be satisfied. I should know that my life was out of my hands. I should know, above all, that my long, long, old, old pain of loneliness would stop, June twenty-seventh, 1903.

I shall die naturally some day—probably after I have grown old and sour. If I have had my Happiness for a year or a day, well and good. I shall be content to grow as old and as sour as the Devil wills. But having had no Happiness— if I find myself growing old and still no Happiness—oh, then I vow I will not live another hour, even if dying were rushing headlong to damnation!

I am, do you see, a philosopher and a coward—with the philosophy of cowardice. I squeeze juice also from this fact sometimes— but the juice is not sweet juice.

The Devil—the fascinating man-devil—it may be, is coming, coming, coming.

And meanwhile I go on and on, in the midst of sand and barrenness.

THE town of Butte presents a wonderful field to a student of humanity and human nature. There are not a great many people—seventy thousand perhaps—but those seventy thousand are in their way unparalleled. For mixture, for miscellany—variedness, Bohemianism—where is Butte's rival?

The population is not only of all nationalities and stations, but the nationalities and stations mix and mingle promiscuously with each other, and are partly concealed and partly revealed in the mazes of a veneer that belongs neither to nation nor to station, but to Butte.

The nationalities are many, it is true, but Irish and Cornish predominate. My acquaintance extends widely among the inhabitants of Butte. Sometimes when I feel in the mood for it I spend an afternoon in visiting about among diverse curious people.

At some Fourth of July demonstration, or on a Miners' Union day, the heterogeneous herd turns out—and I turn out, with the herd and of it, and meditate and look on. There are Irishmen—Kelleys, Caseys, Calahans, staggering under the weight of much whiskey, shouting out their green-isle maxims; there is the festive Cornishman, ogling and leering, greeting his fellow-countrymen with alcoholic heartiness, and gazing after every feminine creature with

lustful eyes; there are Irish women swearing ge-
nially at each other in shrill pleasantry, and five
or six loudly-vociferous children for each; there
are round-faced Cornish women likewise, each
with her train of children; there are suave, sleek
sporting men just out of the bath-tub; insignificant lawyers, dentists, messenger boys; "plung-
ers" without number; greasy Italians from
Meaderville; greasier French people from the
Boulevarde Addition; ancient miners—each of
whom was the first to stake a claim in Butte;
starved-looking Chinamen here and there; a con-
tingent of Finns and Swedes and Germans;
musty, stuffy old Jew pawn-brokers who have
crawled out of their holes for a brief recreation;
dirt-encrusted Indians and squaws in dirty, gay
blankets, from their flea-haunted camp below
the town; "box-rustlers"—who are as common
in Butte as bar-maids in Ireland; swell, flashy-
looking Africans; respectable women with white
aprons tied around their waists and sailor-hats
on their heads, who have left the children at
home and stepped out to see what was going
on; innumerable stray youngsters from the dark
haunts of Dublin Gulch; heavy restaurant-keep-
ers with toothpicks in their mouths; a vast army
of dry-goods clerks—the "paper-collared" gen-
try; miners of every description; representatives
from Dog Town, Chicken Flats, Busterville,
Butchertown, and Seldom Seen—suburbs of

Butte; pale, thin individuals who sing and dance in beer-halls; smart society people in high traps and tallyhos; impossible women—so-called (though in Butte no one is more possible), in vast hats and extremely plaid stockings; persons who take things seriously and play the races for a living; "beer-jerkers"; "biscuit-shooters"; soft-voiced Mexicans and Arabians;—the dregs, the élite, the humbly respectable, the off-scouring—all thrown together, and shaken up, and mixed well.

One may notice many odd bits of irony as one walks among these. One may notice that the Irishmen are singularly carefree and strong and comfortable—and so jolly! while the Irish women are frumpish and careworn and borne earthward with children. The Cornishman who has consumed the greatest amount of whiskey is the most agreeable, and less and less inclined to leer and ogle. The Cornish woman whose profanity is the shrillest and most genial and voluble, is she whose life seems the most weighted and downtrodden. The young women whose bodies are encased in the tightest and stiffest corsets are in the most wildly hilarious spirits of all. The filthy little Irish youngsters from Dublin Gulch are much brighter and more clever in every way than the ordinary American children who are less filthy. A delicate aroma of cocktails and whiskey-and-soda hangs over even the four-in-hands and automobiles of the upper crust. Gamblers, newsboys, and Chinamen are the most chivalrously courteous among them. And the modest-looking "plunger" who has drunk the greatest number of high-balls is the most gravely, quietly polite of all. The rolling, rollicking, musical profanity of the "ould sod"— Bantry Bay, Donegal, Tyrone, Tipperary—falls much less limpidly from the cigaretted lips of the ten-year-old lad than from those of his mother, who taught it to him. One may notice that the husband and wife who smile the sweetest at each other in the sight of the multitudes are they whose countenances bear various scars and scratches commemorating late evening orgies at home; that the peculiar solid, block-shaped appearance of some of the miners' wives is due quite as much to the quantity of beer they drink as to their annual maternity; that the one grand ruling passion of some men's lives is curiosity;—that the entire herd is warped, distorted, barren, having lived its life in smoke-cured Butte.

A single street in Butte contains people in nearly every walk of life—living side by side resignedly, if not in peace.

In a row of five or six houses there will be living miners and their families, the children of which prevent life from stagnating in the street while their mothers talk to each other—with the inevitable profanity—over the back-fences. On the corner above there will be a mysterious widow with one child, who has suddenly alighted upon the neighborhood, stealthily in the night, and is to be seen at rare intervals emerging from her door— the target for dozens of pairs of eager eyes and half as many eager tongues. And when the mysterious widow, with her one child, disappears some night as suddenly and as stealthily as she appeared, an outburst of highly-colored rumors is tossed with astonishing glibness over the various back-fences—all relating to the mysterious widow's shady antecedents and past history, to those of her child, and to the cause of her sudden departure,—no two of which rumors agree in any particular. Across on the opposite corner there will be a company of strange people who also descended suddenly, and upon whom the eyes of the entire block are turned with absorbing interest. They consist of half-a-dozen men and women seemingly bound together only by ties of conviviality. The house is kept closely-blinded and quiet all day, only to burst forth in a blaze of revel in the evening, which revel lasts all night. This goes on until some momentous night, at the request of certain proper ones, a police officer glides quietly into the midst of a scene of unusual gaiety—and the festive company melts into oblivion, never to return. They also are then discussed with rapturous relish and in tones properly lowered, over the back-fences. Farther down the street there will live an interesting being of feminine persuasion who has had five divorces and is in course of obtaining another. These divorces, the causes therefor, the justice thereof, and the future prospects of the multi-grass widow, are gone over, in all their bearings, by the indefatigable tongues.

Every incident in the history of the street is put through a course of sprouts by these same tireless members. The Jewish family that lives in the poorest house in the neighborhood, and that is said to count its money by the hundred thousands; the aristocratic family with the Irish-point curtains in the windows—that lives on the county; the family whose husband and father gains for it a comfortable livelihood forging checks; the miner's family whose wife and mother wastes its substance in diamonds and sealskin coats and other riotous living; the family in extremely straitened circumstances into which new babies arrive in great and distressing numbers; the strange lady with an apoplectic complexion and a wonderfully foul and violent flow of invective—all are discussed over and over and over again. No one is omitted.

And so this is Butte, the promiscuous—the Bohemian. And all these are the Devil's playthings. They amuse him, doubtless.

Butte is a place of sand and barrenness.

The souls of these people are dumb.

ALWAYS I wonder, when I die will there be anyone to remember me with love? I know I am not lovable.

That I want it so much only makes me less lovable, it seems. But—who knows?—it may be there will be some one.

My anemone lady does not love me. How can she—since she does not understand me? But she allows me to love her—and that carries me a long way. There are many—oh, a great many—who will not allow you to love them if you would.

There is no one to love me now. Always I wonder how it will be after some long years when I find myself about to die.

IN THIS house where I drag out my accursed, devilish, weary existence, upstairs in the bathroom, on the little ledge at the top of the wain-scoting, there are six tooth-brushes: an ordinary white bone-handled one that is my younger brother's; a white twisted-handled one that is my sister's; a flat-handled one that is my older brother's; a celluloid-handled one that is my stepfather's; a silver-handled one that is mine; and another ordinary one that is my mother's. The sight of these tooth-brushes day after day, week after week, and always, is one of the most crushingly maddening circumstances in my fool's life.

Every Friday I wash up the bathroom. Usually I like to do this. I like the feeling of the water squeezing through my fingers, and always it leaves my nails beautifully neat. But the obviousness of those six tooth-brushes signifying me and the five other members of this family and the aimless emptiness of my existence here—Friday after Friday—makes my soul weary and my heart sick.

Never does the pitiable, barren, contempt-ible, damnable, narrow Nothingness of my life in this house come upon me with so intense a force as when my eyes happen upon those six tooth-brushes.

Among the horrors of the Inquisition, a minute refinement of cruelty was reached when the victim's head was placed beneath a never-ceasing falling of water, drop by drop.

A convict sentenced to solitary confinement, spending his endless days staring at four blank walls, feels that had he committed every known crime he could not possibly deserve his punishment.

I am not undergoing an Inquisition, nor am I a convict in solitary confinement. But I live in a house with people who affect me mostly through their tooth-brushes—and those I should like, above all things, to gather up and pitch out of the bathroom window—and oh, damn them, *damn* them!

You who read this, can you understand the depth of bitterness and hatred that is contained in this for me? Perhaps you can a little if you are a woman and have felt yourself alone.

When I look at the six tooth-brushes a fierce, lurid storm of rage and passion comes over me. Two heavy leaden hands lay hold of my life and press, press, press. They strike the sick, sick weariness to my inmost soul.

Oh, to leave this house and these people, and this intense Nothingness—oh, to pass out from them, forever! But where can I go, what can I do? I feel with mad fury that I am help-less. The grasp of the stepfather and the mother is contemptible and absurd—but with the persistence and tenacity of narrow minds. It is like the two heavy leaden hands. It is not seen—it is not tangible. It is felt.

Once I took away my own silver-handled tooth-brush from the bathroom ledge, and kept it in my bedroom for a day or two. I thought to lessen the effect of the six.

I put it back in the bathroom.

The absence of one accentuated the significant damnation of the others. There was something more forcibly maddening in the five than in the six tooth-brushes. The damnation was not worse, but it developed my feeling about them more vividly.

And so I put my tooth-brush back in the bathroom.

This house is comfortably furnished. My mother spends her life in the adornment of it. The small square rooms are distinctly pretty.

But when I look at them seeingly I think of the proverb about the dinner of stalled ox.

Yet there is no hatred here, except mine and my bitterness. I am the only one of them whose bitter spirit cries out against things.

But there is that which is subtler and strikes deeper. There is the lack of sympathy—the lack of everything that counts: there is the great, deep Nothing.

How much better were there hatred here than Nothing!

I long hopelessly for will-power, resolution to take my life into my own hands, to walk away from this house some day and never return. I have nowhere to go—no money, and I know the world quite too well to put the slightest faith in its voluntary kindness of heart. But how much better and wider, less damned, less maddening, to go out into it and be beaten and cheated and fooled with, than *this*!—this thing that gathers itself easily into a circle made of six toothbrushes with a sufficiency of surplus damnation.

I have read about a woman who went down from Jerusalem to Jericho and fell among thieves. Perhaps she had a house at Jerusalem with six toothbrushes and Nothingness. In that case she might have rushed gladly into the arms of thieves.

I think of crimes that strike horror and revulsion to my maid-senses. And I think of my Nothingness, and I ask myself were it not better to walk the earth an outcast, a solitary woman, and meet and face even these, than that each and every one of my woman-senses should wear slowly, painfully to shreds, and strain and break—in this unnameable Nothing?

Oh, the dreariness—the hopelessness of Nothing!

There are no words to tell it. And things are always hardest to bear when there are no words for them.

However great one's gift of language may be, there is always something that one can not tell.

I am weary of self—always self. But it must be so.

My life is filled with *self*.

If my soul could awaken fully perhaps I might be lifted out of myself—surely I should be. But my soul is not awake. It is awakening, trying to open its eyes; and it is crying out blindly after something, but it can not *know*. I have a dreadful feeling that it will stay always like this.

Oh, I feel everything—everything! I feel what might be. And there is Nothing. There are six tooth-brushes.

Would I stop for a few fine distinctions, a theory, a natural law even, to escape from this into Happiness—or into something greatly less?

Misery—misery! If only I could feel it less!

Oh, the weariness, the weariness—as I await the Devil's coming.

OFTEN I walk out to a place on the flat valley below the town, to flirt with Death. There is within me a latent spirit of coquetry, it appears.

Down on the flat there is a certain deep, dark hole with several feet of water at the bottom.

This hole completely fascinates me. Sometimes when I start out to walk in a quite different direction, I feel impelled almost irresistibly to turn and go down on the flat in the direction of the fascinating, deep black hole.

And here I flirt with Death. The hole is so narrow—only about four feet across—and so dark, and so deep! I don't know whether it was intended to be a well, or whether it is an abandoned shaft of some miner. At any rate it is isolated and deserted, and it has a rare loving charm for me.

I go there sometimes in the early evening, and kneel on the edge of it and lean over the dark pit, with my hand grasping a wooden stake that is driven into the ground near by. And I drop little stones down and hear them splash hollowly, and it sounds a long way off.

There is something wonderfully soothing, wonderfully comforting to my unrestful, aching wooden heart in the dark mystery of this fascinating hole. Here is the End for me, if I want it—here is the Ceasing, when I want it. And I lean over and smile quietly.

"No flowers," I say softly to myself, "no weeping idiots, no senseless funeral, no oily undertaker fussing over my woman's-body, no useless Christian prayers. Nothing but this deep dark restful grave."

No one would ever find it. It is mile and a half from any house.

The water—the dark still water at the bottom—would gurgle over me and make an end quickly. Or if I feared there was not enough water, I would bring with me a syringe and some morphine and inject an immense quantity into one white arm, and kneel over the tender darkness until my youth-weary, waiting-worn senses should be overcome, and my slim, light body should fall. It would splash into the water at the bottom—it would follow the little stones at last. And the black, muddy water would soak in and begin the destroying of my body, and murky bubbles would rise so long as my lungs continued to breathe. Or perhaps my body would fall against the side of the hole, and the head would lie against it out of the water. Or perhaps only the face would be out of the water, turned upward to the light above—or turned half-down, and the hair would be darkly wet and heavy, and the face would be blue-white below it, and the eyes sink inward.

"The End, the End!" I say softly and ecstatically. Yet I do not lean farther out. My hand does not loosen its tight grasp on the wooden stake. I am only flirting with Death now.

Death is fascinating—almost like the Devil. Death makes use of all his arts and wiles, powerful and alluring, and flirts with deadly temptation for me. And I make use of my arts and wiles—and tempt him.

Death would like dearly to have me, and I would like dearly to have him. It is a flirtation that has its source in mutual desire. We do not love each other, Death and I,—we are not friends. But we desire each other sensually, lustfully.

Sometime I suppose I shall yield to the desire. I merely play at it now—but in an unmistakable manner. Death knows it is only a question of time.

But first the Devil must come. First the Devil, then Death: a deep dark soothing grave—and the early evening, "and a little folding of the hands to sleep."

I AM in no small degree, I find, a sham—a player to the gallery. Possibly this may be felt as you read these analyses.

While all of these emotions are written in the utmost seriousness and sincerity, and are exactly as I feel them, day after day—so far as I have the power to express what I feel—still I aim to convey through them all the idea that I am lacking in the grand element of Truth—that there is in the warp and woof of my life a thread that is false—false.

I don't know how to say this without the fear of being misunderstood. When I say I am in a way a sham, I have no reference to the truths as I have given them in this Portrayal, but to a very light and subtle thing that runs through them.

Oh, do not think for an instant that this analysis of my emotions is not perfectly sincere and real, and that I have not felt all of them more than I can put into words. They are my tears—my life-blood!

But in my life, in my personality, there is an essence of falseness and insincerity. A thin, fine vapor of fraud hangs always over me and dampens and injures some things in me that I value.

I have not succeeded thoroughly in analyzing this—it is so thin, so elusive, so faint—and yet not little. It is a natural thing enough viewed in the light of my other traits.

I have lived my nineteen years buried in an environment at utter variance with my natural instincts, where my inner life is never touched, and my sympathies very rarely, if ever, appealed to. I never disclose my real desires or the texture of my soul. Never, that is to say, to anyone except my one friend, the anemone lady.—And so every day of my life I am playing a part; I am keeping an immense bundle of things hidden under my cloak. When one has played a part— a false part—all one's life, for I was a sly, artful little liar even in the days of five and six; then one is marked. One may never rid oneself of the mantle of falseness, charlatanry— particularly if one is innately a liar.

A year ago when the friendship of my anemone lady was given me, and she would sometimes hear sympathetically some long-silent bit of pain, I felt a snapping of tense-drawn cords, a breaking away of flood-gates—and a strange, new pain. I felt as if I must clasp her gentle hand tightly and give way to the pent-up, surging tears of eighteen years. I had wanted this tender thing more than anything else all my life, and it was given me suddenly.

I felt a convulsion and a melting, within.

But I could not tell my one friend exactly what I felt. There was no doubt in my own mind as to my, own perfect sincerity of feeling, but there was with it and around it this vapor of fraud, a spirit of falseness that rose and confronted me and said, "hypocrite," "fool."

It may be that the spirit of falseness is itself a false thing—yet true or false, it is with me always. I have tried, in writing out my emotions, to convey an idea of this sham element while still telling everything faithfully true. Sometimes I think I have succeeded, and at other times I seem to have signally failed. This element of falseness is absolutely the very thinnest, the very finest, the rarest of all the things in my many-sided character.

It is not the most unimportant.

I have seen visions of myself walking in various pathways. I have seen myself trying one pathway and another. And always it is the same: I see before me in the path, darkening the way and filling me with dread and discouragement, a great black shadow—the shadow of my own element of falseness.

I can not rid myself of it.

I am an innate liar.

This is a hard thing to write about. Of all things it is the most liable to be misunderstood. You will probably misunderstand it, for I have not succeeded in giving the right idea of it. I aimed at it and missed it. It eluded me completely.

You must take the idea as I have just now presented it for what it may be worth. This is as near as I can come to it. But it is something infinitely finer and rarer.

It is a difficult task to show to others a thing which, though I feel and recognize it thoroughly, I have not yet analyzed for myself.

But this is a complete Portrayal of me—as I await the Devil's coming—and I must tell everything—everything.

SO THEN, yes. As I have said, I find that I am quite, quite odd.

My various acquaintances say that I am *funny*. They say, "Oh, it's that May MacLane, Dolly's younger sister. She's funny." But I call it oddity. I bear the hall-mark of oddity.

There was a time, a year or two since, when I was an exceedingly sensitive little fool—sensitive in that it used to strike very deep when my young acquaintances would call me funny and find in me a vent for their distinctly unfriendly ridicule. My years in the high school were not years of joy. Two years ago I had not yet risen above these things. I was a sensitive little fool.

But that sensitiveness, I rejoice to say, has gone from me. The opinion of these young people, or of these old people, is now a thing that is quite unable to affect me.

The more I see of conventionality, it seems, the more I am odd.

Though I am young and feminine—very feminine—yet I am not that quaint conceit, a *girl*: the sort of person that Laura E. Richards writes about, and Nora Perry, and Louisa M. Alcott,—girls with bright eyes, and with charming faces (they always have charming faces), standing with reluctant feet where the brook and river meet, and all that sort of thing.

I missed all that.

I have read some girl-books, a few years ago—"Hildegarde Grahame," and "What Katy Did," and all,—but I read them from afar. I looked at those creatures from behind a high board fence. I felt as if I had more tastes in common with the Jews wandering through the wilderness, or with a band of fighting Amazons. I am not a girl. I am a woman, of a kind. I began to be a woman at twelve, or more properly, a genius.

And then, usually, if one is not a girl one is a heroine—of the kind you read about. But I am not a heroine, either. A heroine is beautiful— eyes like the sea shoot opaque glances from under drooping lids—walks with undulating movements, her bright smile haunts one still, falls methodically in love with a man—always with a man, eats things (they are always called "viands") with a delicate appetite, and on special occasions her voice is full of tears. I do none of these things. I am not beautiful. I do not walk with undulating movements—indeed, I have never seen any one walk so, except, perhaps, a cow that has been overfed. My bright smile haunts no one. I shoot no opaque glances from my eyes, which are not like the sea by any means. I have never eaten any viands, and my appetite for what I do eat is most excellent. And my voice has never yet, to my knowledge, been full of tears.

No, I am not a heroine.

There never seem to be any plain heroines, except Jane Eyre, and she was very unsatisfactory. She should have entered into marriage with her beloved Rochester in the first place. I should have, let there be a dozen mad wives upstairs. But I suppose the author thought she must give her heroine some desirable thing— high moral principles, since she was not beautiful. Some people say that beauty is a curse. It may be true, but I'm sure I should not have at all minded being cursed a little. And I know several persons who might well say the same. But, anyway, I wish some one would write a book about a plain, bad heroine so that I might feel in real sympathy with her.

So far from being a girl or a heroine, I am a thief—as I have before suggested.

I mind me of how, not long since, I stole three dollars. A woman whom I know rather well, and lives near, called me into her house as I was passing and asked me to do an errand for her. She was having an ornate gown made, and she needed some more appliqué with which to festoon it. The appliqué cost nine dollars a yard. My trusting neighbor gave me a bit of the braid for a sample and two twenty-dollar bills. I was to get four yards. I did so, and came back and gave her the braid and a single dollar. The other three dollars I kept myself. I wanted three dollars very much, to put with a few that I already had in my purse. My trusting neighbor is of the kind that throws money about carelessly. I knew she would not pay any attention to a little detail like that,—she was deeply interested in her new frock; or perhaps she would think I had got thirty-nine dollars' worth of appliqué. At any rate, she did not need the money, and I wanted three dollars, and so I stole it.

I am a thief.

It has been suggested to me that I am a kleptomaniac. But I am sure my mind is perfectly sane. I have no such excuse. I am a plain, downright thief.

This is only one of my many peculations. I steal money, or anything that I want, whenever I can, nearly always. It amuses me—and one must be amused.

I have only two stipulations: that the person to whom it belongs does not need it pressingly, and that there is not the smallest chance of being found out. (And of course I could not think of stealing from my one friend.)

It would be extremely inconvenient to be known as a thief, merely.

When the world knows you are a thief it blinds itself completely to your other attributes. It calls you a thief, and there's an end. I am a genius as well as a thief—but the world would quite overlook that fact. "A thief's a thief," says the world. That is very true. But the mere fact of being a thief should not exclude the consideration of one's other traits. When the world knows you are a Methodist minister, for instance, it will admit that you may also be a violinist, or a chemist, or a poet, and will credit you therefor. And so if it condemns you for being a thief, it should at the same time admire you for being a genius. If it does not admire you for being a genius, then it has no right to condemn you for being a thief.

—And why the world should condemn any one for being a thief—when there is not within its confines any one who is not a thief in some way—is a bit of irony upon which I have wasted much futile logic.—

I am not trying to justify myself for stealing. I do not consider it a thing that needs to be justified, any more than walking or eating or going to bed. But, as I say, if the world knew that I am a thief without being first made aware with emphasis that I am some other things also, then the world would be a shade cooler for me than it already is—which would be very cool indeed.

And so in writing my Portrayal I have dwelt upon other things at some length before touching on my thieving propensities.

None of my acquaintances would suspect that I am a thief. I look so respectable, so refined, so "nice," so inoffensive, so sweet, even!

But, for that matter, I am a great many things that I do not appear to be.

The woman from whom I stole the three dollars, if she reads this, will recognize it. This will be inconvenient. I fervently hope she may not read it. It is true she is not of the kind that reads.

But, after all, it's of no consequence. This Portrayal is Mary MacLane: her wooden heart, her young woman's-body, her mind, her soul.

The world may run and read.

I will tell you what I did with the three dollars. In Dublin Gulch, which is a rough quarter of Butte inhabited by poor Irish people, there lives an old world-soured, wrinkled-faced woman. She lives alone in a small, untidy house. She swears frightfully like a parrot, and her reputation is bad—so bad, indeed, that even the old woman's compatriots in Dublin Gulch do not visit her lest they damage their own. It is true that the profane old woman's morals are not good—have never been good—judged by the world's standards. She bears various marks of cold, rough handling on her mind and body. Her life has all but run its course. She is worn out.

Once in a while I go to visit this old woman—my reputation must be sadly damaged by now.

I sit with her for an hour or two and listen to her. She is extremely glad to have me there. Except me she has no one to talk to but the milkman, the grocery man, and the butcher. So always she is glad to see me. There is a certain bond of sympathy between her and me. We are fond of each other. When she sees me picking my way towards her house, her hard, sour face softens wonderfully and a light of distinct friendliness comes into her green eyes.

Don't you know, there are few people enough in the world whose hard, sour faces will soften at sight of you and a distinctly friendly light come into their green eyes. For myself, I find such people few indeed.

So the profane old woman and I are fond of each other. No question of morals, or of immorals, comes between us. We are equals.

I talk to her a little—but mostly she talks. She tells me of the time when she lived in County Galway, when she was young—and of her several husbands, and of some who were not husbands, and of her children scattered over the earth. And she shows me old tin-types of these people. She has told me the varied tale of her life a great many times. I like to hear her tell it. It is like nothing else I have heard. The story in its unblushing simplicity, the sour-faced old woman sitting telling it, and the tin-types,— contain a thing that is absurdly, grotesquely, tearlessly sad.

Once when I went to her house I brought with me six immense, heavy, fragrant chrysanthemums.

They had been bought with the three dollars I had stolen.

It pleased me to buy them for the profane old woman. They pleased her also—not because she cares much for flowers, but because I brought them to her. I knew they would please her, but that was not the reason I gave her them.

I did it purely and simply to please myself.

I knew the profane old woman would not be at all concerned as to whether they had been bought with stolen money or not, and my only regret was that I had not had an opportunity to steal a larger sum so that I might have bought more chrysanthemums without inconveniencing my purse.

But as it was they filled her dirty little dwelling with perfume and color.

Long ago, when I was six, I was a thief— only I was not then, as now, a graceful, light-fingered thief—I had not the philosophy of stealing.

When I would steal a copper cent out of my mother's pocketbook I would feel a dreadful, suffocating sinking in my bad heart, and for days and nights afterwards—long after I had eaten the chocolate mouse—the copper cent would haunt me and haunt me, and oh, how I wished it back in that pocketbook with the clasp shut tight and the bureau drawer locked!

And so, is it not finer to be nineteen and a thief, with the philosophy of stealing—than to be six and haunted day and night by a copper cent?

For now always my only regret is, when I have stolen five dollars, that I did not steal ten while I was about it.

It is a long time ago since I was six.

TO-DAY I walked over the hill where the sun vanishes down in the afternoon.

I followed the sun so far as I could, but two even very good legs can do no more than carry one into the midst of the sunshine—and then one may stand and take leave, lovingly, of it.

I stood in the valley below the hill and looked away at the gold-yellow mountains that rise into the cloudy blue, and at the long gray stretches of rolling sand. It all reminded me of the Devil and the Happiness he will bring me.

Some day the Devil will come to me and say: "Come with me."

And I will answer: "Yes."

And he will take me away with him to a place where it is wet and green—where the yellow, yellow sunshine falls on heaven-kissing hills, and misty, cloudy masses float over the valleys.

And for days I shall be happy—happy—happy!

For *days!* The Devil and I will love each other intensely, perfectly—for days! He will be incarnate, but he will not be a man. He will be the man-devil, and his soul will take mine to itself and they will be one—for days.

Imagine me raised out of my misery and obscurity, dullness and Nothingness, into the full, brilliant life of the Devil—for days!

The love of the man-devil will enter into my barren, barren life and melt all the cold, hard things, and water the barrenness, and a million little green growing plants will start out of it; and a clear, sparkling spring will flow over it—through the dreary, sandy stretches of my bitterness, among the false stony roadways of my pain and hatred. And a great rushing, flashing cataract of melting love will flow over my weariness and unrest and wash it away forever. My soul will be fully awakened and there will be a million little sweet new souls in the green growing things. And they will fill my life with everything that is beautiful—tenderness, and divineness, and compassion, and exaltation, and uplifting grace, and light, and rest, and gentleness, and triumph, and truth, and peace. My life will be borne far out of self, and self will sink quietly out of sight—and I shall see it farther and farther away, until it disappears.

"It is the last—the *last*—of that Mary MacLane," I will say, and I will feel a long, sighing, quivering farewell.

A thousand years of misery—and now a million years of Happiness.

When the sun is setting in the valley and the crests of those heaven-kissing hills are painted violet and purple, and the valley itself is reeking and swimming in yellow-gold light, the man-devil—whom I love more than all—and I will go out into it.

We will be saturated in the yellow light of the sun and the gold light of Love.

The man-devil will say to me: "Look, you little creature, at this beautiful picture of joy and Happiness. It is the picture of your life as it will be while I am with you—and I am with you for days."

Ah, yes, I will take a last, long farewell of this Mary MacLane. Not one faint shadow of her weary wretched Nothingness will remain.

There will be instead a brilliant, buoyant, joyous creature—transformed, adorned, garlanded by the love of the Devil.

My mind will be a treasure-house of art, swept and garnished and strong and at its best.

My barren, hungry heart will come at last to its own. The red flames of the man-devil's love will burn out forever its pitiable, distorted, wooden quality, and he will take it and cherish it—and give me his.

My young woman's-body likewise will be metamorphosed, and I shall feel it developing and filled with myriads of little contentments and pleasures. Always my young woman's-body is a great and important part of me, and when I am married to the Devil its finely-organized nerve-power and intricate sensibility will be culminated to marvelous completeness. My soul—upon my soul will descend consciously the light that never was on land or sea.

This will be for days—for days.

No matter what came before, I will say; no matter what comes afterward. Just now it is the man-devil, my best-beloved, and I, living in the yellow light.

Think of living with the Devil in a bare little house, in the midst of green wetness and sweetness and yellow light—for days!

In the gray dawn it will be ineffably sweet and beautiful, with shining leaves and the gray, unfathomable air, and the wet grass, and all.

"Be happy now, my weary little wife," the Devil will say.

And the long, long yellow-gold day will be filled with the music of Real Life.

My grandest possibility will be realized. The world contains a great many things—and this is my grandest possibility realized!

I will weep rapturous tears.

When I think of all this and write it there is in me a feeling that is more than pain.

Perhaps the very sweetest, the tenderest, the most pitiful and benign human voice in the world could sing these things and this feeling set to their own wondrous music,—and it would echo far—far,—and you would understand.

A T TIMES when I walk among the natural things—the barren, natural things—I know that I believe in Something. Why can I not call it God and pray to it?

There is Something—I do not know it intellectually, but I feel it—I *feel* it—with my soul. It does not seem to reach down to me. It does not pity me. It does not look at me tenderly in my unhappiness.

My soul feels only that it is there.

No. It is not all-loving, all-gracious, all-pitying. It hurts me—it hurts me always as I walk over the sand. But even while it hurts me it seems to promise—ah, those beautiful things that it promises me!

And then the hurting is anguish—for I know that the promises will never be fulfilled.

There is within me a thing that is aching, aching, aching always as the days pass.

It is not my pain of wanting, nor my pain of unrest, nor my pain of bitterness, nor of hatred. I know those in all their own anguish.

This aching is another pain. It is a pain that I do not know—that I feel ignorantly but sharply, and, oh, it is torture, torture!

My soul is worn and weary with pain. There is no compassion—no mercy upon me. There is no one to help me bear it. It is just I alone out on the sand and barrenness. It is cruel anguish to be always alone—and so long—oh, so long!

Nineteen years are as ages to you when you are nineteen.

When you are nineteen there is no experience to tell you that all things have an end.

This aching pain has no end.

I feel no tears now, but I feel heavy sobs that shake my life to its center.

My soul is wandering in a wilderness.

There is a great light sometimes that draws my soul toward it. When my soul turns toward it, it shines out brilliant and dazzling and awful—and the worn, sensitive thing shrinks away, and shivers, and is faint.

Shall my soul have to know this Light, inevitably? Must it, some day, plunge into this?

Oh, it may be—it may be. But I know that I shall die with the pain.

There are times when the great Light is dim and beautiful as the starlight—the utter agony of it—the cruel, ineffable loveliness!

Do you understand this? I am telling you my young, passionate life-agony? Do you listen to it indifferently? Has it no meaning for any one? For me it means everything. For me it makes life old, long, weariness.

It may be that you know. And perhaps you would even weep a little with me if you had time.

It is as if this Light were the light of the Christian religion—and the Christian religion is full of hatred. It says, "Come unto me, you that are heavy laden, and I will give you rest." But when you would go, when you reach up with your weary hands, it sends you a too-brilliant Light—it makes you fair, wondrous promises— it puts you off. You beseech it in your suffering—

"While the waters near me roll,
While the tempest still is high—"

but it does not listen—it does not care. Worship me, worship me, it says, but after that let me alone. There is a bookful of promises. Take it and thank me and worship me.

It does not care.

If I obey it, it looks on indifferently. If I disobey it, it looks on indifferently. If I am in woe, it looks on indifferently. If I am in a brief joy, it looks on indifferently.

I am left all alone—all alone.

The Light is shown me and I reach after it, but it is placed high out of my reach.

I see the promises in the Light. Oh, why— *why* does it promise these things! Is not the burden of life already greater than I can bear? And there is the story of the Christ. It is beautiful. It is damningly beautiful. It draws the tears of pain and soft anguish from me at the sense of beauty.

And when every nerve in me is melted and over-flowing, then suddenly I am conscious that it is a lie—a *lie*.

Everywhere I turn there is Nothing—Nothing.

My soul wails out its grief in loneliness.

My soul wanders hither and thither in the dark wilderness and asks, asks always in blind, dull agony, How long?—how long?

L IFE is a pitiful thing.

STAND in the midst of my sand and barrenness and gaze hard at everything that is within my range of vision—and ruin my eyes trying to see into the darkness beyond.

And nearly always I feel a vague contempt for you, fine, brave world—for you and all the things that I see from my barrenness. But I promise you, if some one comes from among you over the sunset hill one day with love for me, I will fall at your feet.

I am a selfish, conceited, impudent little animal, it is true, but, after all, I am only one grand conglomeration of Wanting—and when some one comes over the barren hill to satisfy the wanting. I will be humble, humble in my triumph.

It is a difficult thing—a most difficult thing—to live on as one year follows another, from childhood slowly to womanhood, without one single sharer of your life—to be alone, always alone, when your one friend is gone. Oh, yes, it is hard! Particularly when one is not high-minded and spiritual, when one's near longing is not a God and a religion, when one wants above all things the love of a human being—when one is a woman, young and all alone. Doubtless you know, this. After all, fine brave world, there are some things that you know very well. Whether or not you care is a quite different matter.

You have the power to take this wooden heart in a tight, suffocating grasp. You have the power to do this with pain for me, and you have the power to do it with ravishing gentleness. But whether or not you will is another matter.

You may think evil of me before you have finished reading this. You will be very right to think so—according to your standards. But sometimes you see evil where there is no evil, and think evil when the only evil is in your own brains.

My life is a dry and barren life. You can change it.

"Oh, the little more, and how much it is! And the little less, and what worlds away."

Yes, you can change it. Stranger things have happened. Again, whether you will—that is a quite different thing.

No doubt you are the people and wisdom will die with you. I do not question that. I will admit and believe anything you may assert about yourselves. I do not want your wisdom, your judgment. I want some one to come up over the barren sunset hill. My thoughts are the thoughts of youth, which are said to be long, long thoughts.

Your life is multi-colored and filled with people. My life is of the gray of sand and barrenness, and consists of Mary MacLane, the longing for Happiness, and the memory of the anemone lady.

This Portrayal is my deepest sincerity, my tears, my drops of red blood. Some of it is wrung from me—wrung by my ambition to tell *everything*. It is not altogether good that I should give you all this, since I do not give it for love of you. I am giving it in exchange for a few gayly-colored things. I want you to know all these passions and emotions. I give them with the utmost freedom. I shall be furious indeed if you do not take them. At the same time, the fact that I am exchanging my tears and my drops of red blood for your gayly-colored trifles is not a thing that thrills me with delight.

But it's of little moment. When the Devil comes over the hill with Happiness I will rush at him frantically headlong—and nothing else will matter.

MARY MACLANE —what are you, you forlorn, desolate little creature? Why are you not of and in the galloping herd? Why is it that you stand out separate against the background of a gloomy sky? Why can you not enter into the lives and sympathies of other young creatures? There have been times when you strained every despairing nerve to do so—before you realized that these things were not for you, that the only sympathy for you was that of Mary MacLane, and the only things for you were those you could take yourself—not which were given you. And your things are few, few, you starved, lean little mud-cat—you worn, youth-weary, obscure little genius!

Oh, it is a wearisome waiting—for the Devil.

TO-DAY when I walked over my sand and barrenness I felt Infinite Grief.

Everything is beyond me.

Nothing is mine.

My single friendship shines brightly before me, and is fascinating—and always just out of my reach.

I want the love and sympathy of human beings, and I repel human beings.

Yes, I repel human beings.

There is something about me that faintly and finely and unmistakably repels.

When my Happiness comes, shall I be able to have it? Shall I ever have anything?

This repellent power is not an outward quality. It is something that comes from deeply, deeply within. It is something that was there in the Beginning. It is a thing from the Original.

There is no ridding myself of it. There is no ridding myself of it. There is no ridding myself of it.

Oh, I am damned—damned!

There is not one soul in the world to feel for me and with me—not one out of all the millions. No one can understand—*no one.*

You are saying to yourself that I imagine this.

What right have you to say so? You don't know anything about me. I know all about me.

I have studied all the elements and phases in my life for years and years. I do not imagine anything. I am even fool enough to shut my eyes to some things until, inevitably, I know I must meet them. I am racked with the passions of youth, and I am young in years. Beyond that I am mature—old. I am not a child in anything but my passions and my years. I feel and recognize everything thoroughly. I have not to imagine anything. My inner life is before my eyes.

There is something about me that no one can understand. Can there ever be any one to understand? Shall I not always walk my barren road alone?

This follows me incessantly. It is burning like a smouldering fire every hour of my life.

Oh, deep black Despair!

How I suffer, how I suffer—just in being alive.

I feel Infinite Grief.

Oh, Infinite Grief—

OFTEN in the early morning I leave my bed and get me dressed and go out into the Gray Dawn. There is something about the Gray Dawn that makes me wish the world would stop, that the sun would never more come up over the edge, that my life would go on and on and rest in the Gray Dawn.

In the Gray Dawn every hard thing is hidden by a gray mantle of charity, and only the light, vague, caressing fancies are left.

Sometimes I think I am a strange, strange creature—something not of earth, nor yet of heaven, nor of hell. I think at times I am a little thing fallen on the earth by mistake: a thing thrown among foreign, unfitting elements, where there is nothing in touch with it, where life is a continual struggle, where every little door is closed—every Why unanswered, and itself knows not where to lay its head. I feel a deadly certainty in some moments that the wild world contains not one moment of rest for me, that there will never be any rest, that my woman's-soul will go on asking long, long centuries after my woman's-body is laid in its grave.

I felt this in the Gray Dawn this morning, but the gray charitable mantle softened it. Always I feel most acutely in the Gray Dawn, but always there is the thing to soften it.

The gray atmosphere was charged. There was a tense electrical thrill in the cold, soft air. My nerves were keenly alive. But the gray curtain was mercifully there. I did not feel too much.

How I wished the yellow, beautiful sun would never more come up over the edge to show me my nearer anguish!

"Stay with me, stay with me, soft Gray Dawn," implored every one of my tiny lives. "Let me forget. Let the vanity, the pain, the longing sink deep and vanish—all of it, all of it! And let me rest in the midst of the Gray Dawn.

I heard music—the silent music of myriad voices that you hear when all is still. One of them came and whispered to me softly: "Don't suffer any more just now, little Mary MacLane. You suffer enough in the brightness of the sun and the blackness of the night. This is the Gray Dawn. Take a little rest."

"Yes," I said, "I will take a little rest."

And then a wild, swelling chorus of voices whispered in the stillness: "Rest, rest, rest, little Mary MacLane. Suffer in the brightness, suffer in the blackness—your soul, your wooden heart, your woman's-body. But now a little rest—a little rest."

"A little rest," I said again.

And straightway I began resting lest the sun should come too quickly over the edge.

When I have heard in summer the wind in a forest of pines, blowing a wondrous symphony of purity and truth, my varied nature felt itself abashed and there was a sinking in my wooden heart. The beauty of it ravished my senses, but it savored crushingly of the virtue that is far above and beyond me, and I felt a certain sore, despairing grief.

But the Gray Dawn is in perfect sympathy. It is quite as beautiful as the wind in the pines, and its truth and purity are extremely gentle, and partly hidden under the gray curtain.

Almost I can be a different Mary MacLane out in the Gray Dawn. Let me forget all the mingled agonies of my life. Let me walk in the midst of this soft grayness and drink of the waters of Lethe.

The Gray Dawn is not Paradise; it is not a Happy Valley; it is not a Garden of Eden; it is not a Vale of Cashmere. It is the Gray Dawn— soft, charitable, tender. "The brilliant celestial yellow will come soon," it says; "you will suffer then to your greatest extent. But now I am here—and so, rest."

And so in the Gray Dawn I was forgetting for a brief period. I was submerged for a little in Lethe, river of oblivion. If I had seen some one coming over the near horizon with Happiness I should have protested: Wait, wait until the gray Dawn has passed.

The deep, deep blue of the summer sky stirs me to a half-painful joy. The cool green of a swiftly-flowing river fills my heart with unquiet longings. The red, red of the sunset sky convulses my entire being with passion. But the dear Gray Dawn brings me Rest.

Oh, the Gray Dawn is sweet—sweet!

Could I not die for very love of it!

The Gray Dawn can do no wrong. If those myriad voices suddenly had begun to sing a volumptuous evil song of the so great evil that I could not understand, that I could feel instantly, still the Gray Dawn would have been fine and sweet and beautiful.

Always I admire Mary MacLane greatly— though sometimes in my admiration I feel a complete contempt for her. But in the Gray Dawn I love Mary MacLane tenderly and passionately.

I seem to take on a strange, calm indifference to everything in the world but just Mary MacLane and the Gray Dawn. We two are identified with each other and joined together in shadowy vagueness from the rest of the world.

As I walked over my sand and barrenness in the Gray Dawn a poem ran continuously through my mind. It expressed to me in my gray condition an ideal life and death and ending. Every desire of my life melted away in the Gray Dawn except one good wish that my own life

and death might be short and obscure and complete like them. The poem was this beautiful
one of Charles Kingsley's:

> " 'Oh, Mary, go and call the cattle home,
>   And call the cattle home,
>   And call the cattle home,
>   Across the sands of Dee!'
> The western wind was wild and dank with
>   foam,
>   And all alone went she.
>
> "The creeping tide came up along the sand,
>   And o'er and o'er the sand,
>   And round and round the sand,
>   As far as eye could see;
> The blinding mist came up and hid the
>   land—
>   And never home came she.
>
> "Oh, is it weed, or fish, or floating hair?—
>   A tress of golden hair,
>   Of drowned maiden's hair,
>   Above the nets at sea.
> Was never salmon yet that shone so fair
>   Among the stakes on Dee.
>
> "They rowed her in across the rolling foam,
>   The cruel, crawling foam,
>   The cruel, hungry foam,
>   To her grave beside the sea;
> But still the boatmen hear her call the cattle
>   home
>   Across the sands of Dee."

This is a poem perfect. And in the Gray Dawn it expresses to me a most desirable thing— a short, eventless life, a sudden ceasing, and a forgotten voice sometimes calling. This Mary, in the Gray Dawn, would wish nothing else. If the waters rolled over me now—over my short, eventless life—there would be the sudden ceasing,—and the anemone lady would hear my voice sometimes, and remember me—the anemone lady and one or two others. And after a short time even my pathetic, passionate voice would sound faint and be forgotten, and my world of sand and barrenness would know me and my weary little life—tragedy no more.

And well for me, I say,—in the Gray Dawn.

It is different—oh, very different—when the yellow bursts through the gray. And the yellow is with me all day long, and at sunset—the red, red line!

Yet—oh, sweet Gray Dawn!

SOMETIMES I am seized with nearer, vivider sensations of love for my one friend, the anemone lady.

She is so dear—so beautiful!

My love for her is a peculiar thing. It is not the ordinary woman-love. It is something that burns with a vivid fire of its own. The anemone lady is enshrined in a temple on the inside of my heart that shall always only be hers.

She is my first love—my only dear one.

The thought of her fills me with a multitude of feelings, passionate yet wonderfully tender,—with delight, with rare, undefined emotions, with a suggestion of tears.

Oh, dearest anemone lady, shall I ever be able to forget your beautiful face! There may be some long, crowded years before me; it may be there will be people and people entering and departing—but, oh, no—no, I shall never forget! There will be in my life always—always the faint sweet perfume of the blue anemone: the memory of my one friend.

Before she went away, to see her, to be near her, was an event in my life—a coloring of the dullness. Always when I used to look at her there would rush a train of things over my mind, a vaguely glittering pageant that came only with her, and that held an always-vivid interest for me.

There were manifold and varied treasures in this train. There were skies of spangled sapphire, and there were lilies, and violets wet with dew. There was the music of violins, and wonderful weeds from the deep sea, and songs of troubadours, and gleaming white statues. There were ancient forests of oak and clematis vines; were lemon-trees, and fretted palaces, and moss-covered old castles with moats and draw-bridges and tiny mullioned windows with diamond panes. There was a cold, glittering cataract of white foam, and a little green boat far off down the river, drifting along under drooping willows. There was a tree of golden apples, and a banquet in a beautiful house with the melting music of lutes and harps, and mulled orange-wine in tall, thin glasses. There was a field of long, fine grass, soft as bat's-wool, and there were birds of brilliant plumage—scarlet and indigo with gold-tipped wings.

All these and a thousand fancies alike vaguely glittering would rush over me when I was with the anemone lady. Always my brain was in a gentle delirium. My nerves were unquiet.

It was because I love her.

Oh, there is not—there can never be—another anemone lady!

My life is a desert—a desert, but the thin, clinging perfume of the blue anemone reaches to its utter confines. And nothing in the desert is the same because of that perfume. Years will not fade the blue of the anemone, nor a thousand bitter winds blow away the rare fragrance.

I feel in the anemone lady a strange attraction of sex. There is in me a masculine element that, when I am thinking of her, arises and overshadows all the others.

"Why am I not a man," I say to the sand and barrenness with a certain strained, tense passion, "that I might give this wonderful, dear, delicious woman an absolutely perfect love!"

And this is my predominating feeling for her.

So, then, it is not the woman-love, but the man-love, set in the mysterious sensibilities of my woman-nature. It brings me pain and pleasure mingled in that odd, odd fashion.

Do you think a man is the only creature with whom one may fall in love?

Often I see coming across the desert a long line of light. My soul turns toward it and shrinks away from it as it does from all the lights. Some day, perhaps, all the lights will roll into one terrible white effervescence and rush over my soul and kill it. But this light does not bring so much of pain, for it is soft and silvery, and always with it is the Soul of Anemone.

THERE are several things in the world for which I, of womankind and nineteen years, have conceived a forcible repugnance—or rather, the feeling was born in me; I did not have to conceive it.

Often my mind chants a fervent litany of its own that runs somewhat like this:

From women and men who dispense odors of musk; from little boys with long curls; from the kind of people who call a woman's figure her "shape": Kind Devil, deliver me.

From all sweet girls; from "gentlemen"; from feminine men: Kind Devil, deliver me.

From black under-clothing—and any color but white; from hips that wobble as one walks; from persons with fishy eyes; from the books of Archibald C. Gunter and Albert Ross: Kind Devil, deliver me.

From the soft persistent, maddening glances of water-cart drivers: Kind Devil, deliver me.

From lisle-thread stockings; from round, tight garters; from brilliant brass belts: Kind Devil, deliver me.

From insipid sweet wine; from men who wear moustaches; from the sort of people that call legs "limbs"; from bedraggled white petticoats: Kind Devil, deliver me.

From unripe bananas; from bathless people;

from a waist-line that slopes up in the front: Kind Devil, deliver me.

From an ordinary man; from a bad stomach, bad eyes, and bad feet: Kind Devil, deliver me.

From red note-paper; from a rhinestone-studded comb in my hair; from weddings: Kind Devil, deliver me.

From cod-fish balls; from fried eggplant, fried beef-steak, fried porkchops, and fried French toast: Kind Devil, deliver me.

From wax flowers off a wedding-cake, under glass; from thin-soled shoes; from tape-worms; from photographs perched up all over my house: Kind Devil, deliver me.

From soft old bachelors and soft old widowers; from any masculine thing that wears a pale blue necktie; from agonizing elocutionists who recite "Curfew Shall Not Ring To-Night," and "The Lips That Touch Liquor Shall Never Touch Mine"; from a Salvation Army singing hymns in slang: Kind Devil, deliver me.

From people who persist in calling my good body "mere vile clay"; from idiots who appear to know all about me and enjoin me not to bathe my eyes in hot water since it hurts their own; from fools who tell me what I "want" to do: Kind Devil, deliver me.

From a nice young man; from tin spoons; from popular songs: Kind Devil, deliver me.

From pleasant old ladies who tell a great

many uninteresting, obvious lies; from men with watch-chains draped across their middles; from some paintings of the old masters which I am unable to appreciate; from side-saddles: Kind Devil, deliver me.

From the kind of man who sings, "Oh, Promise Me!"—who sings at it; from constipated dressmakers; from people who don't wash their hair often enough: Kind Devil, deliver me.

From a servant girl with false teeth; from persons who make a regular practice of rubbing oily mixtures into their faces; from a bed that sinks in the middle: Kind Devil, deliver me.

And so on and on and on. And in each petition I am deeply sincere. But, kind Devil, only bring me Happiness and I will more than willingly be annoyed by all these things. Happiness for two days, kind Devil, and then, if you will, languishing widowers, lisle-thread stockings—anything, for the rest of my life.

And hurry, kind Devil, pray—for I am weary.

I T IS astonishing to me how very many contemptible, petty vanities are lodged in the crevices of my genius. My genius itself is one grand good vanity—but it is not contemptible. And even those little vanities—though they are contemptible, I do not hold them in contempt by any means. I smile involuntarily at their absurdness sometimes, but I know well that they have their function.

They are peculiarly of my mind, my humanness, and they are useful therein. When this mind stretches out its hand for things and finds only wilderness and Nothingness all about it, and draws the hand back empty, then it can only turn back—like my soul—to itself. And it finds these innumerable little vanities to quiet it and help it. My soul has no vanity, and it has nothing, nothing to quiet it. My soul is wearing itself out, eating itself away. These vanities are a miserable substitute for the rose-colored treasures that it sees a great way off and even imagines in its folly that it may have, if it continues to reach after them. Yet the vanities are something. They prevent my erratic, analytical mind from finding a great Nothing when it turns back upon itself.

If I were not so unceasingly engrossed with my sense of misery and loneliness my mind would produce beautiful, wonderful logic. I am a genius—a genius—a genius. Even after all this you may not realize that I am a genius. It is a hard thing to show. But, for myself, I feel it. It is enough for me that I feel it.

I am not a genius because I am foreign to everything in the world, nor because I am intense, nor because I suffer. One may be all of these and yet not have this marvelous perceptive sense. My genius is because of nothing. It was born in me as germs of evil were born in me. And mine is a genius that has been given to no one else. The genius itself enables me to be thoroughly convinced of this.

It is hopeless, never-ending loneliness!

My ancestors in their Highlands—some of them—were endowed with second sight. My genius is not in the least like second sight. That savors of the supernatural, the mysterious. My genius is a sound, sure, earthly sense, with no suggestion of mystery or occultism. It is an inner sense that enables me to feel and know things that I could not possibly put into thought, much less into words. It makes me know and analyze with deadly minuteness every keen, tiny damnation in my terrible lonely life. It is a mirror that shows me myself and something in myself in a merciless brilliant light, and the sight at once sickens and maddens me and fills me with an unnamed woe. It is something unspeakably dreadful. The sight for the time deadens all thought in my mind. It freezes my reason and intellect. Logic can not come to my aid. I can only feel and know the thing and it analyzes itself before my eyes.

I am alone with this—alone, alone, alone! There is no pitiful hand extended from the height—there is no human being—ah, there is Nothing.

How can I bear it! Oh, I ask you—how can I bear it!

MY GENIUS is an element by itself, and it is not a thing that I can tell in so many words. But it makes itself felt in every point of my life. This book would be a very different thing if I were not a genius— though I am not a literary genius. Often people who come in contact with me and hear me utter a few commonplace remarks feel at once that I am extraordinary.

I am extraordinary.

I have tried longingly, passionately, to think that even this sand and barrenness is mine. But I can not. I know beyond the shadow of a doubt that it, like all good things, is beyond me. It has something that I also have. In that is our bond of sympathy.

But the sand and barrenness itself is not mine.

Always I think there is but one picture in the world more perfect in its art than the picture of me in my sand and barrenness. It is the picture of the Christ crucified with two thieves. Nothing could be more divinely appropriate. The art in it is ravishingly perfect. It is one of the few perfect pictures set before the world for all time. As I see it before my mind I can think only of its utter perfectness. I can summon no feeling of grief at the deed. The deed and the art are perfect. Its perfectness ravishes my senses.

And within me I feel that the picture of me in my sand and barrenness—knowing that even the sand and barrenness is not mine—is only second to it.

SOMETIMES when I go out on the barrenness my mind wanders afar. To-day it went, to Greece.

Oh, it was very beautiful in Greece!

There was a wide, long sky that was vividly, wonderfully blue. And there was a limitless sea that was gray and green. And it went far to the south. The sky and the sea spread out into the vast world—two beautiful elements, and they fell in love with each other. And the farther away they were the nearer they moved together until at last they met and clasped each other in the far distance. There were tall, dark-green trees of kinds that are seen only in Greece. They murmured and whispered in the stillness. The wind came off from the sea and went over them and around them. They quivered and trembled in shy, ecstatic joy—for the wind was their best-beloved. There were banks of moss of a deep emerald color, and golden flowers that drooped their heavy sensual heads over to the damp black earth. And they also loved each other, and were with each other, and were glad. Clouds hung low over the sea and were dark-gray and heavy with rain. But the sun shone from behind them at intervals with beams of bronze-and-copper. Three white rocks rose up out of the sea, and the bronze-and-copper beams fell upon them, and straightway were of gold.

Oh, how beautiful were those three gold rocks that came up out of the sea!

Aphrodite once came up out of this same sea. She came gleaming, with golden hair and beautiful eyes. Her skin glowed with tints of carmine and wild rose. Her white feet touched the smooth, yellow sand on the shore. The white feet of Aphrodite on the yellow sand made a picture of marvelous beauty. She was flushed in the joy of new life.

But the bronze-and-copper sunshine on the three white rocks was more beautiful than Aphrodite.

I stood on the shore and looked at the rocks. My heart contracted with the pain that beautiful things bring.

The bronze-and-copper in the wide gray and green sea!

"This is the gateway of Heaven," I said to myself. "Behind those three gold rocks there is music and the high notes of happy voices." My soul grew faint. "And there is no sand and barrenness there, and no Nothingness, and no bitterness, and no hot, blinding tears. And there are no little heart-weary children, and no lonely young women—oh, there is no loneliness at all!" My soul grew more and more faint with thinking of it. "And there is no heart there but that is pure and joyous and in Peace—in long, still, eternal Peace. And every life comes there to its own; and every earth-cry is answered, and every earth-pain is ended; and the dark spirit of Sorrow that hangs always over the earth is gone— gone,—beyond the gateway of Heaven. And more than all, Love is there and walks among the dwellers. Love is a shining figure with radiant hands, and it touches them all with its hands so that never-dying love enters into their hearts. And the love of each for another is like the love of each for self. And here at last is Truth. There is searching and searching over the earth after Truth—and who has found it? But here is it beyond the gateway of Heaven. Those who enter in know that it is Truth at last."

And so Peace and Love and Truth are there behind the three gold rocks. And then my soul could no longer endure the thought of it.

Suddenly the sun passed behind a heavy, dark-gray cloud, and the bronze-and-copper faded from the three rocks and left them white— very white in the wide water.

The yellow flowers laid their heads drowsily down on the emerald moss. The wind from off the sea played very gently among the motionless branches of the tall trees. The blue, blue sky and the wide, gray-green sea clasped each other more closely and mingled with each other and became one vague, shadowy element—and from it all I brought my eyes back thousands of leagues to my sand and barrenness.

The sand and barrenness is itself an element, and I have known it a long, long time.

EVERYTHING is so dreary—so dreary. I feel as if I would like to die to-day. I should not be the tiniest bit less unhappy afterward—but this life is unutterably weary. I am not strong. I can not bear things. I do not want to bear things. I do not long for strength. I want to be happy.

When I was very little, it was cold and dreary also, but I was certain it would be different when I should grow and be ten years old. It must be very nice to be ten, I thought,—and one would not be nearly so lonesome. But when the years passed and I was ten it was just exactly as lonesome. And when I was ten everything was very hard to understand.

But it will surely be different when I am seventeen, I said. I will know so much when I am seventeen. But when I was seventeen it was even more lonely, and everything was still harder to understand.

And again I said—faintly—everything will become clearer in a few years more, and I will wonder to think how stupid I have always been. But now the few years more have gone and here I am in loneliness that is more hopeless and harder to bear than when I was very little. Still, I wonder indeed to think how stupid I have been—and now I am not so stupid. I do not tell myself that it will be different when I am five-and-twenty.

For I know that it will not be different.

I know that it will be the same dreariness, the same Nothingness, the same loneliness.

It is very, very lonely.

It is hope deferred and maketh the heart sick.

It is more than I can bear.

Why—*why* was I ever born!

I can not live, and I can not die—for what is there after I am dead? I can see myself wandering in dark and lonely places.

Yet I feel as if I would like to die to-day.

IF IT were pain alone that one must bear, one could bear it. One could lose one's sense of everything but pain.

But it is pain with other things. It is the sense of pain with the sense of beauty and the sense of the anemone. And there is that mysterious pain.

Who knows the name of that mysterious pain?

It is these mingled senses that torture me.

I HAVE been placed in this world with eyes to see and ears to hear, and I ask for Life. Is it to be wondered at? Is it so strange? Should I be content merely to see and to hear? There are other things for other people. Is it atrocious that I should ask for some other things also?

Is thy servant a dog?

IN THESE days of approaching emotional Nature even the sand and barrenness begins to stir and rub its eyes.

My sand and barrenness is clothed in the awful majesty of countless ages. It stands always through the never-ending march of the living and the dead. It may have been green once—green and fertile, and birds and snakes and everything that loves green growing things may have lived in it. It may have sometime been rolling prairie. It may have been submerged in floods. It changed and changed in the centuries. Now it is sand and barrenness, and there are no birds and no snakes; only me. But whatever change came to it, whatever its transfiguration, the spirit of it never moved. Flood, or fertility, or rolling prairie, or barrenness—it is only itself. It has a great self, a wonderful self.

I shall never forget you, my sand and barrenness.

Some day, shall my thirsty life be watered, my starved heart fed, my asking voice answered, my tired soul taken into the warmth of another with the intoxicating sweetness of love?

It may be.

But I shall remember the sand and the barrenness that is with me in my Nothingness. The sand and barrenness and the memory of the anemone lady are all that are in any degree mine.

And so then I shall remember it.

As I stand among the barren gulches in these days and look away at the slow-awakening hills of Montana, I hear the high, swelling, half-tired, half-hopeful song of the world. As I listen I know that there are things, other than the Virtue and the Truth and the Love, that are not for me. There is beyond me, like these, the unbreaking, undying bond of human fellowship—a thing that is earth-old.

It is beyond me, and it is nothing to me.

In my intensest desires—in my widest longings—I never go beyond *self*. The ego is the all.

Limitless legions of women and men in weariness and in joy are one. They are killing each other and torturing each other, and going down in sorrow to the dust. But they are one. Their right hands are joined in unseen sympathy and kinship.

But my two hands are apart, and clasped together in an agony of loneliness.

I have read of women who have been strongly, grandly brave. sometimes I have dreamed that I might be brave. The possibilities of this life are magnificent.

To be saturated with this agony, I say at times, and to bear with it all; not to sink beneath it, but to vanquish it, and to make it the grace and comeliness of my entire life from the Beginning to the End!

Perhaps a woman—a real woman—could do this.

But I?—No. I am not real—I do not seem *real* to myself. In such things as these my life is a blank.

There was Charlotte Corday—a heroine whom I admire above all the heroines. And more than she was a heroine she was a woman. And she had her agony. It was for love of her fair country.

To suffer and do and die for love of something! It is glorious! What must be the exalted ecstasy of Charlotte Corday's soul now!

And I—with all my manifold passions—I am a coward.

I have had moments when, vaguely and from far off, it seemed as if there might be bravery and exaltation for me,—when I could rise far over myself. I have felt unspeakable possibilities. While they lasted—what wonderful emotion was it that I felt?

But they are not real.

They fade away—they fade away.

And again come the varied phenomena of my life to bewilder and terrify me.

Confusion! Chaos! Damnation!

They are not moments of exaltation now. Poor little Mary MacLane!

"If to do were as easy as to know what

were good to do, chapels had been churches, and poor men's cottages princes' palaces."

I do not know what to do.

I do not know what were good to do.

I would do nothing if I knew.

I might add to my litany this: Most kind Devil, deliver me—from myself.

TO-DAY I walked over the sand, and it was almost beautiful.

The sun was sinking and the sky was filled with roses and gold.

Then came my soul and confronted me. My soul is wondrous fair. It is like a young woman. The beauty of it is too great for human eyes to look upon. It is too great for mine. Yet I look.

My soul said to me: "I am sick."

I answered: "And I am sick."

"We may be well," said my soul. "Why are we not well?"

"How may we be well?" I asked.

"We may throw away all our vanity and false pride," said my soul. "We may take on a new life. We may learn to wait and to possess ourselves in patience. We may labor and overcome."

"We can do none of these things," I cried. "Have I not tried all of them some time in my short life? And have I not waited and wanted until you have become faint with pain? Have I not looked and longed? Dear soul, why do you not resign yourself? Why can you not stay quiet and trouble yourself and me no more? Why are you always straining and reaching? There isn't anything for you. You are wearing yourself out."

My soul made answer: "I may strain and reach until only one worn nerve of me is left.

And that one nerve may be scourged with whips and burned with fire. But I will keep one atom of faith. I may go bad, but I will keep one atom of faith in Love and in the Truth that is Love. You are a genius, but I am no genius. The years—a million of years—may do their utmost to destroy the single nerve. They may lash and beat it. I will keep my one atom of faith. "You are not wise," I said. "You have been wandering and longing for a time that seems a thousand years—through my cold, dark childhood to my cold, dark womanhood. Is that not enough to quiet you? Is that not enough to teach you the lesson of Nothing? You are not a genius, but you are not a fool."

"I will keep my one atom of faith," said my soul.

"But lie and sleep now," I said. "Don't reach after that Light any more. Let us both sleep a few years."

"No," said my soul.

"Oh, my soul," I wailed, "look away at that glowing copper horizon—and beyond it. Let us go there now and take an infinite rest. Now! We can bear this no longer."

"No," said my soul; "we will stay here and bear more. There would be no rest yet beyond the copper horizon. And there is no need of going anywhere. I have my one atom of faith."

I gazed at my soul as it stood plainly before me, weak and worn and faint, in the fading light. It had one atom of faith, it said, and tried to hold its head high and to look strong and triumphant. Oh, the irony—the pathos of it! My soul, with its one pitiful atom of faith, looked only what it was—a weeping, hunted thing.

IN SOME rare between-whiles it is as if nothing mattered. My heart aches, I say; my soul wanders; this person or that person was repelled today; but nothing matters.

A great inner languor comes like a giant and lays hold of me. I lie fallow beneath it.

Some one forgot me in the giving of things. But it does not matter. I feel nothing.

Persons say to me, don't analyze any more and you will not be unhappy.

When Something throws heavy clubs at you and you are hit by them, don't be hurt. When Something stronger than you holds your hands in the fire, don't let it burn you. When Something pushes you into a river of ice, don't be cold. When something draws a cutting lash across your naked shoulders, don't let it concern you—don't be conscious that it is there.

This is great wisdom and fine, clear logic.

It is a pity that no one has ever yet been able to live by it.

But after all it's no matter. Nothing is any one's affair. It is all of no consequence.

And have I not had all my anguish for nothing? I am a fool—a fool.

A handful of rich black mud in a pig's yard—does it wonder why it is there? Does it torture itself about the other mud around it, and about the earth and water of which it is made, and about the pig? Only fool's mud would do so. And so, then, I am fool's mud.

Nothing counts. Nothing can possibly count.

Regret, passion, cowardice, hope, bravery, unrest, pain, the love-sense, the soul-sense, the beauty-sense—all for nothing! What can a handful of rich black mud in a pig's yard have to do with these? I am a handful of rich black mud— a fool-woman, fool's mud.

All on earth that I need to do is to lie still in the hot sun and feel the pig rolling and floundering and slushing about. It were folly to waste my mud nerves in wondering. Be quiet, fool-woman, let things be. Your soul is a fool's-mud soul and is governed by the pig; your heart is a fool's-mud heart, and wants nothing beyond the pig; your life is a fool's-mud life, and is the pig's life.

Something within me shrieks now, but I do not know what it is—nor why it shrieks.

It groans and moans.

There is no satisfaction in being a fool—no satisfaction at all.

BUT yes. It all matters, whether or no. Nature is one long battle, and the never-ending perishing of the weak. I must grind and grind away. I have no choice. And I must know that I grind.

Fool, genius, young lonely woman—I must go round and round in the life within, for how many years the Devil knows. After that my soul must go round and round, for how many centuries the Devil knows.

What a master-mind is that of the Devil! The world is a wondrous scheme. For me it is a scheme that is black with woe. But there may be in the world some one who finds it beautiful Real Life.

I wonder as I write this Portrayal if there will be one person to read it and see a thing that is mingled with every word. It is something that you must feel, that must fascinate you, the like of which you have never before met with.

It is the unparalleled individuality of me.

I wish I might write it in so many words of English. But that is not possible. If I have put it in every word and if you feel it and are fascinated, then I have done very well.

I am marvelously clever if I have done so.

I know that I am marvelously clever. But I have need of all my peculiar genius to show you my individuality—my aloneness.

I am alone out on my sand and barrenness. I should be alone if my sand and barrenness were crowded with a thousand people each filled with melting sympathy for me—though it would be unspeakably sweet.

People say of me, "She's peculiar. They do not understand me. If they did they would say so oftener and with emphasis.

And so I try to put my individuality in the quality of my diction, in my method of handling words.

My conversation plainly shows this individuality—more than shows it, indeed. My conversation hurls it violently at people's heads. My conversation—when I choose—makes people turn around in their chairs and stare and give me all of their attention. They admire me, though their admiration is mixed decidedly with other feelings.

I like to be admired.

It soothes my vanity.

When you read this Portrayal you will admire me. You will surely have to admire me.

And so this is life, and everything matters.

But just now I will stop writing and go downstairs to my dinner. There is a porterhouse steak, broiled rare, and some green young onions. Oh, they are good! And when one is to have a porterhouse steak for one's dinner—and some green young onions, one doesn't give a tupenny dam whether anything else matters or not.

O N A day when the sky is like lead and a dull, tempestuous wilderness of gray clouds adds a dreariness to the sand, there is added to the loneliness of my life a deep bitterness of gall and wormwood.

Out of my bitterness it is easy for bad to come.

Surely Badness is a deep black pool wherein one may drown dullness and Nothingness.

I do not know Badness well. It is something material that seems a great way off now, but that might creep nearer and nearer as I became less and less young.

But now when the day is of the leaden dullness I look at Badness and long for it. I am young and all alone, and everything that is good is beyond my reach. But all that is bad—surely that is within the reach of every one.

I wish for a long pageant of bad things to come and whirl and rage through this strange leaden life of mine and break the spell.

Why should it not be Badness instead of Death? Death, it seems, will bring me but a change of agony. Badness would perhaps so crowd my life with its vivid phenomena that they would act as a neurotic to the racked nerves of my Nothingness. It would be an outlet—and possibly I could forget some things.

I think just now of a woman who lived long ago and in whom the world at large seems not

to have found anything admirable. I mean
Messalina Valeria, the wife of the stupid emperor
Claudius. I have conceived a profound admiration
for this historic wanton. She may not indeed
have had anything to forget; she may not have
suffered. But she had the strength of will to take
what she wanted, to do as she liked, to live as
she chose to live.

It is admirable and beautiful beyond
expression to sacrifice and give up and wait for
love of that good that gives in itself a just
reward. And only next to this is the throwing to
the winds of all restraint when the good holds
itself aloof and gives nothing. We are weak,
contemptible fools who do not grasp the
resources within our reach when there is no just
reward for our restraint. Why do we not take
what we want of the various temptations? It is
not that we are virtuous. It is that we are
cowards.

And it is worth while to remain true to an
ideal that offers only the vaguest hopes of
realization? It is not philosophy. When one has
made up one's mind that one wants a dish of
hot stewed mushrooms, and set one's heart on
it, should one scorn a handful of raw evaporated
apples, if one were starving, for the sake of the
phantom dish of hot stewed mushrooms? Should
one say, Let me starve, but I will never descend
to evaporated apples; I will have nothing but a

dish of hot stewed mushrooms? If one is sure
one will have the stewed mushrooms finally,
before one dies of starvation, then very well.
One should wait for them and take nothing else.

But it is not in my good peripatetic
philosophy to pass by the Badness that the gods
provide for the sake of a faraway, always-
unrealized ideal, however brilliant, however
beautiful, however golden.

When the lead is in the sky and in my life, a
vision of Badness looms up on the horizon and
looks at me and beckons with a fascinating
finger. Then I say to myself, What is the use of
this unsullied, struggling soul; this unbesmirched,
empty heart; this treasureless, innocent mind;
this insipid maid's-body? There are no good
things for them. But here, to be sure, are
fascinating, glittering bad things—the goods that
the gods provide, the compensation of the Devil.

Comes Death, some day, I said—but to die,
in the sight of glittering bad things—and I only
nineteen! These glittering things appear fair.

There is really nothing evil in the world.
Some things appear distorted and unnatural
because they have been badly done. Had they
been perfect in conception and execution they
would strike one only with admiration at their
fine, iridescent lights. You remember Don Juan
and Haidee. That, to be sure, was not evil in
any event—they loved each other. But if they

had had only a passing, if intense, fancy for one another, who would call it evil? Who would call it anything but wonderful, charming, enchanting? The Devil's bad things—like the Devil's good things—may gleam and glisten, oh, how they may gleam and glisten! I have seen them do so, not only in a poem of Byron's, but in the life that is.

Always when the lead is in the sky I would like to cultivate thoroughly this branch of the vineyard. Now doesn't it make you shiver to think of this dear little Mary MacLane wandering unloved through dark by-ways and deadly labyrinths? It makes me shiver. But it needn't. If I am to wander unloved, why not as well wander there as through Nothingness?

I fancy it must be wonderfully easy to become used to the many-sided Badness. I have lived my nineteen years in the midst of Nothingness, and I have not yet become used to it. It has sharp knives in it, has Nothingness. Badness may have some sharp knives also—but there are other things. Yes, there are other things.

Kind Devil, if you are not to fetch me Happiness; then slip off from your great steel key-ring a bright little key to the door of the glittering, gleaming bad things, and give it me, and show me the way, and wish me joy.

I would like to live about seven years of judicious Badness, and then Death, if you will.

Nineteen years of damnable Nothingness, seven years of judicious Badness—and then Death. A noble ambition! But might it not be worse? If not that, then nineteen years of damnable Nothingness, and then Death. No; when the lead is in the sky that does not appeal to me. My versatile mind turns to the seven years of judicious Badness.

There is nothing in the world without its element of Badness. It is in literature; it is in every art—in pictures, sculpture, even in music. There are certain fine, deep, minute passages in Beethoven and in Chopin that tell of things wonderfully, sublimely bad. Chopin one can not understand. Is there any one in the world who can understand him? But we know at once that there is the Badness—and it is music!

There is the element of Badness in me.

I long to cultivate my element of Badness. Badness compared to Nothingness is beautiful. And so, then, I wait also for some one to come over the hill with things other than Happiness. But whatever I wait for, nothing comes.

THERE were pictures in the red sunset sky to-day. I looked at them and was racked with passions of desire. I fancied to myself that I could have any of the good things in the pictures for the asking and the waiting. The while I knew that when the sunset should fade from the sky I would be overwhelmed by my heaviest woe.

There was a picture of intense peace. There were stretches of flat, green country, and oak-trees and aspens, and a still, still lake. In the dim distance you could see fields of wheat and timothy-grass that moved a little as if in the wind. You could fancy the cows feeding just below the brow of the near hills, and a hawk floating and wheeling among the clouds. A rainbow arched over the lake. There is nothing lacking here, I thought. "Life and health and peace possessing." Give me this, kind Devil.

There was a picture of endless, limitless strength. There were the oak-trees again but bereft now of every leaf, and, the bristling, jagged rocks back of them were not more coldly staunch. The sun poured brilliantly bright upon them. A river flowed unmoved and quiet between yellow clay banks. A tornado might sweep over this and not one twig would be displaced, not one ripple would come to the river. Is it not fine! I said to myself. No feeling, no self-analysis, no aching, no pain—and the strength of the Philistines. Oh, kind Devil, I entreat you, let me have that!

There was a picture of untrammeled revel and forgetfulness. There were fields of swaying daffodils and red lilies. The young shrubs tossed their heads and were joyous. Lambs gamboled and the happy meadow-lark knew whereof she sang.

> "The winds with wonder-whist
> Smoothly the waters kissed."

Be carefree, be light-hearted, be wicked—above all, forget. The deeds are what you will; the time is now; the aftermath is nothing; the day of reckoning is never. Love things lightly, take all that you see, and to the winds with regret! Gracious Devil, I whispered intensely, give me this and no other!

There was a picture of raging elements. "The winds blew, and the rains descended and the floods came." The sky was overcast with rolling clouds. The air was heavy with unrest. There was a gray stone house set upon a rocky point, and I had momentary glimpses of an unquiet sea below it. Back on the surface of the land slender trees were waving wildly in the gale. The wind and the rain were saying, "Damn you, little earth, I have you now,—I will rend and ruin you." They whipped and raged in frenzied joy.

The little earth liked it. The elements whirled and whistled round the gray stone house. A lurid light came from a ghastly moon between clouds. The entire scene was desolately savage and forlorn, but attractive. As I listened in fancy to that shrieking, wailing wind, and saw green branches jerked and twisted asunder in the storm, my barren, defrauded heart leaped and exulted. If I could live in the midst of this and be beaten and shaken roughly, would not that deep sense forget to ache? Kind Devil, pray send me some storms. It is Nothingness that bears down heavy.

There was a picture of an exalted spiritual life. There was that strange bright light. And the things in the picture were those things alone in this world that are real, and the only things that count. The old, soft green of the old, old rolling hills was the green of love—the earth-love and the love that comes from beyond the earth. The air and the blue water and the sunshine were so beautifully real and true that except for their deep-reaching, passionate tenderness human strength could not endure them. There were lanes of climbing vines and white violets. Was it my fancy that brought their thin fragrance to me over piles of billowy clouds? There was something there that was old—old as the race. Those green valleys were the same as when the mists first lifted from the earth. As I looked my life stood still. My soul shivered faintly. As I looked I felt nearer, my God, to thee—though I have no God and everything is away from me, nothing tender comes to me.

Still it was nearer, my God, to thee.

A voice came out of the far, far distant ages and said very gently: "All these shadows are falling in vain. You are blinded and bewildered in the darkness—the darkness is deep—deep. There is not one dim ray of light. Your feet falter and stumble. You can not see. But the shadows are falling in vain."

I ask you, Why is this life not mine?

I implore and wring my hands in agonized entreaty, and almost it seems sometimes my fingers can grasp these things—but there is something cold and strong between them and me. Oh, what is it!

There was a picture of various castles in Spain. They were most beautiful, were those castles. The lights that shone on the battlements were soft, bright lights. For one thing, I fancied I saw myself and Fame with me. Fame is very fine. The sun and moon and stars may go dark in the Heavens. Bitter rain may fall out of the clouds. But never mind. Fame has a sun and moon and gently brilliant stars of her own, and these, shining once, shine always. The green river may run dry in the land. But Fame has a green river that never runs dry. One may wander over the face of the earth. But Fame is herself a refuge. One may be a target for stones and mud. Yes—but Fame stands near with her arm laid across one's shoulders—as no other arm can be laid across one's shoulders. Fame would fill several empty places. Fame would continue to fill them for some years.

Fame, if you please, Devil.

There was a picture of Death. I saw a figure lying in the midst of a desert that was rather like my sand and barrenness. Not far off a wolf sat on his haunches and waited for the end. A buzzard perched near and waited also. They both appeared hungry. It seemed as though the end might come quickly.

Let it come, kind Devil.

And a wolf and a buzzard are better than an undertaker and some worms. Although that doesn't much matter.

And oh, there again was the dearest picture of all—the red, red picture of Happiness for me, Happiness with the sunshine falling on the Heaven-kissing hills! There was I, and I loved and was loved. I—out of loneliness into perfect Happiness! The yellow-gold of the glorious hot sun melted and poured over the earth and over everything that was there. The river ran and rippled and sang the most sweetly glad song that ever river sang. Winged things sparkled in the gold light and flew down the sky. "The wonderful air was over me; the wonderful wind was shaking the tree." The silent voices in the air rang out like flutes and clarionets. And the love of the man-devil for me was everywhere—above me, around me, within me. It would last for a number of beautiful yellow-gold days. I—out of the anguish of loneliness into this!

My heart is filled with desire.

My soul is filled with passion.

My life is a life of longing.

All pictures fade before this picture. They fade completely. When the sun itself faded I gazed over my sand and barrenness with blurred, unseeing eyes and wished only with a heavy, desolate spirit for the coming of the Devil.

SOME people think, absurdly enough, that to be Scotch or descended from the Scottish clans is to be rather strong, rather conservative, firm in faith, and all that. The idea is one that should be completely exploded by this time. I think that the Scotch as a nation are the most difficult of all to characterize. Their traits and tendencies cover a wider field than those of any other. To be Scotch is to be anything. There is no man so narrow as a Scotchman. There is no man so broad as a Scotchman. There is no mind so versatile as a Scotch mind. At the same time only a Scotch mind is capable of clinging with bull-dog tenacity to one idea. A Scotch heart out of all, and through all, can be true as death. A Scotch heart—the same one—can be cunning and treacherous as false human hearts are made. To be English is to have limits; the Germans, the French, the Russians—they have all some inevitable attributes to modify their genius.

But one may be anything—anything, if one is Scotch.

Always I think of the cruel, hardened, ferocious, weather-beaten, kilted Clan MacLean wandering over bleak winter hills, fighting the powerful MacDonalds and MacGregors—and generally wiping them from the earth,—marching away with merrily shrieking pipes from fields of withered, blood-soaked heather—and all this merely to gather intensified life for me. I feel that the causes of my tragedy began long, long ago from remote germs.

My Scotch blood added to my genius sense has made me into a dangerous chemical compound. By analyzing I have brought an almost clear portrait of myself up before my mind's eyes.

When I was a child I did not analyze knowingly, but the child was this same genius, though I am one of the kind that changes widely and decidedly in the years. This weary unhappiness is not a matter of development.

When I was a child I felt dumbly what I feel now less dumbly. At the age of five I used sometimes to weep silently in the night—I did not know why. It was that I felt my aloneness, my foreignness to all things. I felt the heavy, heavy weight of life—and I was only five.

I was only five, and it seems a thousand years ago. But sometimes back through the long, winding, unused passages of my mind I hear that silent sobbing of the child and the unarmed wailing of a tiny, tired soul.

It mingles with the bitter Nothingness of the grown young woman, and oh, with it all—with it all I am so unhappy!

There is something subtly *Scotch* in all this.

But Scotch or Indian or Japanese, there is no stopping of the pain.

I FEAR, do you know, fine world, that you do not yet know me really well—particularly me of the flesh. Me of the peculiar philosophy and the unhappy spirit you know rather well by now, unless you are stupider than I think you are. But you might pass me in the street—you might spend the day with me—and never suspect that I am I. Though for the matter of that, even if I had set before you a most graphic and minutely drawn portrait of myself, I am certainly clever enough to act a quite different role if I chose—when you came to spend the day. Still, if the world at large is to know me as I desire it to know me without ever seeing me, I shall have to bring myself into closer personal range with it—and you may rise in your seats and focus your opera-glasses, stare with open mouths, stand on your hind-legs and gape—I will myself turn on glaring green and orange lights from the wings.

I believe that it's the trivial little facts about anything that describe it the most effectively. In "Vanity Fair," when Beckey Sharpe was describing young Crawley in a letter to her friend Amelia, she stated that he had hay-colored whiskers and straw-colored hair. And knowing this you feel that you know much more about the Crawley than you would if Miss Sharpe had not mentioned those things. And yet it is but a mere matter of color!

When you think that Dickens was extremely fond of cats you feel at once that nothing could be more fitting. Somehow that marvelously mingled humor and pathos and gentle irony seem to go exceedingly well with a fondness for soft, green-eyed, purring things. If you had not read the pathetic humor, but knew about Dickens and his warm feline friends you might easily expect such things from him.

When you read somewhere that Dr. Johnson is said never to have washed his neck and his ears, and then go and read some of his powerful, original philosophy, you say to yourself, "Yes, I can readily believe that this man never troubled himself to wash his neck and his ears." I, for my part, having read some of the things he has written, can not reconcile myself to the fact that he ever washed any part of his anatomy. I admire Dr. Johnson—though I wash my own neck occasionally.

When you think of Napoleon amusing himself by taking a child on his knee and pinching it to hear it cry, you feel an ecstatic little wave of pleasure at the perfect fitness of things. You think of his hard, brilliant, continuous victories, and you suspect that Napoleon Bonaparte lived but to gratify Napoleon Bonaparte. When you think of the heavy, muscular man smilingly pinching the child, you are quite sure of it. Such a method of amusement for that king among men is so exquisitely appropriate that you wonder why you had not thought of it yourself.

So, then, yes. I believe strenuously in the efficacy of seemingly trivial facts as portrayers of one's character—one's individual humanness.

Now I will set down for your benefit divers and varied observations relative to me—an interesting one of woman-kind and nineteen years, and curious and fascinating withal.

Well, then.

Nearly every day I make me a plate of hot, rich fudge, with brown sugar (I should be an entirely different person if I made it with white sugar—and the fudge would not be nearly so good), and take it upstairs to my room, with a book or a newspaper. My mind then takes in a part of what is contained in the book or the newspaper, and the stomach of the MacLane takes in all of what is contained in the plate. I sit by my window in a miserable, uncomfortable, stiff-backed chair, but I relieve the strain by resting my feet on the edge of the low bureau. Usually the book that I read is an old dilapidated bound volume of that erstwhile periodical, "Our Young Folks." It is a thing that possesses a charm for me. I never grow tired of it. As I eat my nice brown little squares of fudge I read about a boy whose name is Jack Hazard and who, J.T. Trowbridge informs the reader, is doing his best, and who seems to find it somewhat difficult. I believe I could repeat pages of J.T. Trowbridge from memory, and that ancient bound volume has become a part of my life. I stop reading after a few minutes, but I continue to eat—and gaze at the toes of my shoes which need polishing badly, or at the conglomeration of brilliant pictures on my bedroom wall, or out of the window at the children playing in the street. But mostly I gaze without seeing, and my versatile mind is engaged either in nothing or in repeating something over and over, such as, "But the sweet face of Lucy Gray will never more be seen." Only I am not aware that I have been repeating it until I happen to remember it afterward.

Always the fudge is very good, and I eat and eat with unabated relish until all the little squares are gone. A very little of my fudge has been known to give some people a most terrific stomach-ache—but my own digestive organs seem to like nothing better. It's so brown—so rich!

I amuse myself with this for an hour or two in the afternoon. Then I go downstairs and work awhile.

There are few things that annoy me so much as to be called a young lady. I am no lady—as any one could see by close inspection, and the phrase has an odious sound. I would rather be called a sweet little thing, or a fallen woman, or a sensible girl—though they would each be equally a lie.

Always I am glad when night comes and I can sleep. My mind works busily repeating things while I divest myself of my various dusty garments. As I remove a dozen or two of hairpins from my head I say within me:

"You are old, father William, one would
        hardly suppose
That your eye is as steady as ever;
Yet you balanced an eel on the end of your
        nose—
What made you so awfully clever?"

Always I take a little clock to bed with me and hang it by a cord at the head of my bed for company. I have named the clock Little Fido, because it is so constant and ticks always. It is beginning to stand in the same relation to me as J.T. Trowbridge's magazine. If I were to go away from here I should take Little Fido and the magazine with me.

Every morning, being beautifully hungry after my walk, I eat three boiled eggs out of the shell for my breakfast. The while I mentally thank the kind Providence that invented hens. Also I eat bits of toast. I have my breakfast alone—because the rest of the family are still sleeping,—sitting at a corner of the kitchen table.

I enjoy those three eggs and those bits of toast. Usually when I am eating my breakfast I am thinking of three things: the varying price of any eggs that are fit to eat; of what to do after I've finished my housework and before lunch; and of my one friend. And I meditatively and gently kick the leg of the table with the heel of my right foot.

I have beautiful hair.

In the front of my shirt-waist there are nine cambric handkerchiefs cunningly distributed. My figure is very pretty, to be sure, but not so well developed as it will be in five years—if I live so long. And so I help it out materially with nine cambric handkerchiefs. You can see by my picture that my waist curves gracefully out. Only it is not all flesh—some of it is handkerchief. It amuses me to do this. It is one of my petty vanities.

Likewise by an ingenious arrangement of my striped moreen petticoat I contrive to display a more evident pair of hips than Nature seems to have intended for me at this stage. Doubtless they also will take on fuller proportions when some years have passed. Still I am not dissatisfied with them as they are. It is not as if they were too well developed—in which case I should have need of all my skill in arranging my moreen petticoat so as to lessen their effect. It is easy enough to add on to these things, but one would experience serious difficulty in attempting to take from them. I hate that heavy, aggressive kind of hips. Moreover, small, graceful ones are desirable when one is nineteen. The world at large judges you more leniently on that account—usually. Narrow, shapely hips may give one an effect of youth and harmlessness which is a distinct advantage, when, for instance, one is writing a Portrayal and so will be at the world's mercy. I believe I should not think of attempting to write a Portrayal if I had hips like a pair of saddle-bags. Certainly it would avail me nothing.

Sometimes I look at my face in a mirror and find it not plain but ugly. And there are other times when I look and find it not pretty but beautiful with a Madonna-like sweetness.

I told you I might say more about the liver that is within me before I have done. Well, then, I will say this: that the world, if it had a liver like mine, would be very different from what it is. The world would be many-colored and mobile and passionate and nervous and high-strung and intensely alive and poetic and romantic and philosophical and egotistic and pathetic, and, oh, racked to the verge of madness with the spirit of unrest—if the world had a liver like mine. It is not all of these now. It is rather stupid. Gods and little fishes! Would not the world be wonderful if all in it were like me? And it would be if it had a liver like mine. For it is my liver mostly that makes me what I am—apart from my genius. My liver is fine and perfect, but sensitive, and, well—it's a dangerous thing to have within you.

It is the liver of the MacLanes.

It is the foundation of the curious castle of my existence.

And after all, fine, brave, stupid world, you may be grateful to the Devil that yours is not like it.

I have seventeen little engraved portraits of Napoleon that I keep in one of my bureau-drawers. Often late in the evening, between nine and ten o'clock, when I come in from a walk over the sand and barrenness, I take these pictures from the drawer and gaze at them carefully a long time and think of that man until I am stirred to the depths.

And then easily and naturally I fall in love with Napoleon.

If only he were living now, I think to myself, I would make my way to him by whatever means and cast myself at his feet. I would entreat him with the most passionate humbleness of spirit to take me into his life for three days. To be the wife of Napoleon for three days—that would be enough for a lifetime! I would be much more than satisfied if I could get three such days out of life.

I suppose a man is either a villain or a fool, though some of them seem to be a judicious mingling of both. The type of the distinct villain is preferable to a mixture of the two, and to a plain fool. I like a villain anyway—a villain that can be rather tender at times. And so, then, as I look at the pictures I fall in love with the incomparable Napoleon. The seventeen pictures are all different and all alike. I fall in love with each picture separately.

In one he is ugly and unattractive—and strong. I fall in love with him.

In another he is cruel and heartless and utterly selfish—and strong. I fall in love with him.

In a third he has a fat, pudgy look, and is quite insignificant—and strong. I fall in love with him.

In a fourth he is grandly sad and full of despair—and strong. I fall in love with him.

In the fifth he is greasy and greedy and common-looking—and strong. I fall in love with him.

In the sixth he is masterly and superior and exalted—and strong. I fall in love with him.

In the seventh he is romantic and beautiful—and strong. I fall in love with him.

In the eighth he is obviously sensual and reeking with uncleanness—and strong. I fall in love with him.

In the ninth he is unearthly and mysterious and unreal—and strong. I fall in love with him.

In the tenth he is black and sullen-browed, and ill-humored—and strong. I fall in love with him.

In the eleventh he is inferior and trifling and inane—and strong. I fall in love with him.

In the twelfth he is rough and ruffianly and uncouth—and strong. I fall in love with him.

In the thirteenth he is little and wolfish and vile—and strong. I fall in love with him.

In the fourteenth he is calm and confident and intellectual—and strong. I fall in love with him.

In the fifteenth he is vacillating and fretful and his mouth is like a woman's—and still he is strong. I fall in love with him.

In the sixteenth he is slow and heavy and brutal—and strong. I fall in love with him.

In the seventeenth he is rather tender—and strong. I fall vividly in love with him.

Napoleon was rather like the Devil, I think as I sit in the straight-backed chair with my feet on the bureau and gaze long and intently at the seventeen pictures, late in the evening.

Then I wearily put them away, maddened with the sense of Nothingness, and take Little Fido and go to bed.

Sometimes, early in the evening just before dinner, I sit in the stiff-backed chair with my elbows on the window-sill and my head resting on one hand, and I look out of the window at a Pile of Stones and a Barrel of Lime. These are in the vacant lot next to this house.

I fix my eyes intently on the Pile of Stones and the Barrel of Lime. And I fix my thoughts on them also. And some of my widest thoughts come to me then.

I feel an overwhelming wave of a kind of pantheism which, at the moment I feel it, begins slowly to grow less and less and continues in this until finally it dwindles to a Pile of Stones and a Barrel of Lime.

I feel at the moment that the universe is a Pile of Stones and a Barrel of Lime. They alone are the Real Things.

Take anything at any point and deceive yourself into thinking that you are happy with it. But look at it heavily; dig down underneath the layers and layers of rose-colored mists and you will find that your Thing is a Pile of Stones and a Barrel of Lime.

A struggle or two, a fight, an agony, a passing—and then the only Real Things: a Pile of Stones and a Barrel of Lime.

Damn everything! Afterward you will find that you have done all your damning for naught. For there is nothing worthy of damnation except a Pile of Stones and a Barrel of Lime—and they are not damnable. They have never harmed you, and moreover they alone are the Real Things.

Julius Caesar made many wars. Sir Francis Drake went sailing over the seas. It was all child's play and counts for nothing. Here are the Pile of Stones and a Barrel of Lime.

And so this is how it is early in the evening just before dinner, when I sit in the uncomfortable chair with my elbows on the window-sill and my head resting on one hand.

I have two pictures of Marie Bashkirtseff high upon my wall. Often I lean my head on the back of the chair with my feet on the bureau—always with my feet on the bureau—and look at these pictures.

In one of them she is eighteen years old and wears a green frock which is extremely becoming—of which fact the person inside of it seems fully aware.

The other picture is taken from her last photograph, when she was twenty-four.

Marie Bashkirtseff is a very beautiful creature. And evidently *she* is not obliged to arrange a moreen petticoat over her plumpness. She was a wonderfully voluptuous look for a woman of eighteen years. In the later picture vanity is written in every line of her graceful form and in every feature of that charming face. The picture fairly yells: "I am Marie Bashkirtseff—and, oh, I am splendid!"

And as I look at the pictures I am glad. For though she was admirable and splendid, and all, she was no such genius as I. She had a genius of her own, it is true. But the Bashkirtseff, with her voluptuous body and her attractive personality, is after all a bit ordinary. My genius, though not powerful, is rare and deep, and no one has ever had or ever will have a genius like it.

Mary MacLane, if you live—if you live, my darling, the world will one day recognize your genius. And when once the world has recognized such genius as this—oh, then no one will ever think of profaning it by comparing it with any Bashkirtseff!

But I would give up this genius eagerly, gladly—at once and forever—for one dear, bright day free from loneliness.

The portraits of the Bashkirtseff are certainly beautiful, but there is something about them that is—well, not common, but bourgeois at least, as if she were a German waitress of unusual appearance, or an aristocratic shop-girl, or a nurse with good taste who would walk out on pleasant forenoons wheeling a go-cart— something of that sort. Perhaps it is because her neck is too short, or because her wrists are too muscular-looking. I thank a gracious Devil as I look up at the pictures that I have not those particular points and that particular bourgeois air. I am bound to confess that I have one of my own, but mine is Highland Scotch—and anyway, I am Mary MacLane.

Marie Bashkirtseff is beautiful enough, however, that she can easily afford to look rather second-rate.

I like to look at my two pictures of her.

I value money literally for its own sake. I like the feeling of dollars and quarters rubbing softly together in my hand. Always it reminds me lovely chestfuls of gold that Captain Kidd buried—no one seems to know just where. Usually I keep some fairly-clean dollars and quarters to handle. "Money is so nice!" I say to myself.

If you think, fine world, that I am always interesting and striking and admirable, always original, showing up to good advantage in a company of persons, and all—why, then you are beautifully mistaken. There are times, to be sure, when I can rivet the attention of the crowd heavily upon myself. But mostly I am the very least among all the idiots and fools. I show up to the poorest possible advantage.

Of several ways that are mine there is one that gives me a distinct and hopeless air of insignificance. I have seen people, having met me for the first time, glance carelessly at me as if they were quite sure I had not an idea in my brain—if I had a brain; as if they wondered why I had been asked there; as if they were fully aware that they had but to fiddle and "It" would dance. Sometimes before this highly intellectual gathering breaks up I manage to make them change their minds with astonishing suddenness. But nearly always I don't bother about it at all. I go among people occasionally because it amuses me. It may be a literary club where they talk theosophy, or it may be a cornish dance where they have pasty and saffron cake and the chief amusement is sending beer-bottles at various heads, or it may be a lady-like circle of married women with cerise silk drop-skirts and white kid gloves, drinking chocolate in the afternoon and talking about something "shocking!"

And often, as I say, I am the least of them.

Genius is an odd thing.

When certain of my skirts need sewing, they don't get sewed. I simply pin the rents in them together and it lasts as long or longer than if I had seated myself in my stiff-backed chair with a needle and thread and mended them—like a sensible girl. (I hate a sensible girl.)

Though I have never yet hurriedly pinned up a torn flounce or several inches of skirt-binding without saying softly to myself, using a trite, expressive phrase, "Certainly, it's a hell of a way to do." Still I never take a needle and mend my garments. I couldn't, anyway. I never learned to sew, and I don't intend ever to learn. It reminds me too much of a constipated dressmaker.

And so I pin up the torn places—though, as I say, I never fail to make use of the quaint, expressive phrase.

All of which a reasonably astute reader will recognize as an important point in the portraying of any character—whether mine or the queen of Spain's.

I had for my dinner to-day some whole-wheat bread, some liver-and-bacon, and some green, green early asparagus. While I was eating these the world seemed a very nice place indeed.

I never see people walking along on the opposite side of the street, as I sit by my window, without wondering who they are, and how they live, and how ugly they would look if their bodies were not adorned with clothes. Always I feel certain that some of them are bow-legged.

And sometimes I see a woman in a fearful state of deshabille walk across the vacant lot next to this. "A plague on me," I say then to myself, "if I ever become middle-aged and if my entire being seems to tip up in the front, and if I go about with no stays so that when I tie an apron around my waist my upper fatness hangs over the band like a natural blouse."

And so—I could go on writing all night these seemingly trivial but really significant details relating to the outer genius. But these will answer. These to any one who knows things will be a revelation.

Sometimes you know things, fine brave world.

You must know likewise that though I do ordinary things, when I do them they cease to be ordinary. I make fudge—and a sweet girl makes fudge, but there are ways and ways of doing things. This entire affair of the fudge is one of my uniquest points.

No sweet girl makes fudge and eats it, as I make fudge and eat it.

So it is.

But, oh—who is to understand all this? Who will understand any of this Portrayal? My unhappy soul has delved in shadows far, far beyond and below.

MY PHILOSOPHY, I find after very little analysis, approaches precariously near to sensualism. It is wonderful how many sides there can be to just one character.

Nature, with all those suns, and all those hilltops, and all those rivers, and all those stars, is inscrutable—intangible—maddening. It affects one with unutterable joy and anguish, but no one can ever begin to understand what it means.

Human nature is yet more inscrutable—and nothing appears on the surface. One can have no idea of the things buried in the minds of one's acquaintances. And mostly they are fools and have no idea themselves of what germs are in themselves—of what they are capable. And in most minds it is true the dormant devils never awaken and never are known.

It is another sign of my analytical genius, that I, aged nineteen, recognize the devils in my character. I have not the slightest wish, since things are as they are with me, to rid myself of them. There is in me much more of evil than of good. Genius like mine must needs have with it manifold bad. "I have in me the germ of every crime." I have no desire to destroy these germs. I should be glad indeed to have them develop into a ravaging disease. Something in this dreadful confusion would then give way. My wooden heart and my soul would cry out in the darkness less heavily, less bitterly.

They want something—they know not what.

I give them poison.

They snatch it and eat it hungrily. Then they are not so hungry. They become quieter.

The ravaging disease soothes them to sleep—it descends on them like rain in the autumn.

When I hurry over my sand and barrenness my vivid passions come to me—or when I sit and look at the horizon. When I walk slowly I consider calmly the question of how much evil I should need to kill off my finer feelings, to poison thoroughly this soul of unrest and this wooden heart so that they would never more be conscious of too-brilliant lights, and to make myself over into a quite different creature.

A little evil would do—a little of a fine, good quality.

I should like a man to come (it is always a man, have you ever noticed?—whatever one contemplates when one is of womankind and young). I should like a man to come, I said calmly to myself to-day as I walked slowly over my barrenness—a perfect villain to come and fascinate me and lead me with strong, gentle allurements to what would be technically termed my ruin. And as the world views such things it would be my ruin. But as I view such things it would not be ruin. It would be a new lease on life.

Yes, I should like a man to come—any man so that he is strong and thoroughly a villain, and so that he fascinates me. Particularly he must fascinate me. There must be no falling in love about it. I doubt if I could fascinate him, but I should ask him, quite humbly to lead me to my ruin.

I have never yet seen the man who would not readily respond to such an appeal.

This villain would be no exception.

I would then jerk my life out of this Nothingness by the roots. Farewell, a long farewell, I would say. Then I would go forth with the man to my ruin. The man would be bad to his heart's core. And after living but a short time with him my shy, sensitive soul would be irretrievably poisoned and polluted. The defilement of so sacred and beautiful a thing as marriage is surely the darkest evil that can come to a life. And so everything within me that had turned toward that too-bright light would then drink deep of the lees of death.

The thirst of this incessant unrest and longing, this weariness of self, would be quenched completely.

My life would be like fertile soil planted thickly with rank wild mustard. On every square inch of soil there would be a dozen sprouts of wild mustard. There would be no room—no room at all—for an anemone to grow. If one should start up, instantly it would be choked and overrun with wild mustard. But no anemone would start up.

My life now is a life of pain and revolt.

My life darkened and partly killed would be more than content to drift along with the current.

Oh, it would be a rest!

The Christians sing, there is rest for the weary, on the other side of Jordan, where the tree of life is blooming. But that rest, of course, is for the Christians. My rest will have to come on this side of Jordan. Let the impress of a thoroughly evil and strong man be stamped upon my inner life, and I am convinced there would come a wonderful settled quiet over it. Its spirit would be broken. It would rest. Why not? I have no virtue-sense. Nothing to me is of any consequence except to be rid of this unrest and pain. Yes, surely I might rest.

The coming of the man-devil would bring rest. But I am fool enough to think that marriage—the real marriage—is possible for me!

This other thing is within the reach of every one—of fools and geniuses alike—and of all that come between.

And so I want a fascinating wicked man to come and make me positively, rather than negatively, wicked. I feel a terrific wave of utter weariness. My life lies fallow. I am tired of sitting here. The sand and barrenness is gray with age. And I am gray with age.

Happiness—the red of the sunset sky—is the intensest desire of my life.

But I will grasp eagerly anything else that is offered me—*anything*.

The poisoning of my soul—the passing of my unrest—would rouse my mental power. My genius would receive a wonderful impetus from it. You would marvel, good world, at the things I should write. Not that they would be exalted—not that they would surge upward. Do men gather grapes of thorns or figs of thistles? But they would be marvels of fire and intensity. I should no longer exhaust much of my energy in grinding, grinding within. The things that would come of the thorns and thistles would excite your astonishment and admiration, though they be not grapes and figs.

And as for me—the real me—the creature imbued with a spirit of intense femininity, with a spirit of an intense sense of Love—with a spirit like that of the Magdalene who loved too much, with the very soul of unrest and Nothingness—this thing would vanish swiftly into oblivion, and I should go down a dark world and feel not.

ONE of the remarkable points about my life is that it is so completely, hopelessly alone—a lonely, lonely life. This book of mine contains but one character—myself.

There is also the Devil—as a possibility.

And there is also the anemone lady—my dearest beloved—as a memory.

I have read books that were written to portray but one character, and there were various people brought in to help in the portraying. But my one friend is gone, and there is no person who enters into my inner life in the very least. I am always alone. I might mingle with people intimately every hour of my life—still I should be alone. Always alone—alone.

Not even a God to worship.

How do I bear this? How do I get through the days and days?

And, oh, when it all comes over me, what frightful rage—what long agony of my breaking heart—what utter woe!

When the stars shine down upon me with cold hatred; when miles and miles of barrenness stretch out around me and envelop me in their weary, weary Nothingness; when the wind blows over me like the breath of a vicious giant; when the ugly, ugly sun radiates centuries of hard, heavy bitterness around me from its stinging rays; when the sky maddens me with its cold, careless blue; when the rivers that are flowing over the earth send echoes to me of their hateful voices; when I hear wild geese honking in bitter wailing melody; when bristling edges of jagged rocks cut sharply into my tired life; when drops of rain fall on me and pierce me like steel points; when the voices in the air shriek little-minded malice in my ears; when the green of Nature is the green of spitefulness and cruelty; when the red, red of the setting sun burns and consumes me with its horrid feverish effervescence; when I feel the all-hatred of the Universe for its poor little earth-bugs: then it is that I approach nearest to Rest.

The softnesses are my Unrest.

I do not want those bitter things.

But I must have them if I would rest.

I want the softnesses and I want Rest!

Oh, dear faint soul, it is hard—hard for us.

We are sick with loneliness.

NOW and again I have torturing glimpses of a Paradise. And I feel my soul in its pain every moment of my life. Otherwise, how gladly would I deny the existence of a soul and a life to come!

For my soul is beset with Nothingness, and the Paradise that shows itself is not for me.

HATRED, after all, is the easiest thing of all to bear.

If you have been forgotten by the one who must have made you, and if you have been left alone of human beings all your life—all your nineteen years—then, when at last you see some one looking toward you with beautiful eyes, and extending to you a beautiful hand, and showing you a beautiful heart wherein is just a little of beautiful sympathy for you—for you—oh, that is harder than anything to bear. Harder than the loneliness and the bitterness—and the tears are nearer and nearer.

But one would be hurt often, often for the sake of the beautiful things. Yes, one would gladly be hurt long and often.

I shall never forget how it was with me when I first saw the beautiful eyes of my dearest anemone lady when they were looking gently— at me—and the beautiful hand, and the beautiful heart.

The awakening of my racked soul is hardly more heavily laden with passion and pain. I shall never forget.

Though I feel away from her also, she is the only one out of all to look gently at me.

Let me writhe and falter with pain; let me go mad—but oh, worldful of people—for the love of your God—give me out of this seething darkness only one beautiful human hand to touch mine with *love*, one beautiful human heart to know the aching sad loneliness of mine, one beautiful, human soul to mingle with mine in long, long Rest.

Oh, for a human being, my soul wails—a human being to love me!

Oh, to know—just once—what it is to be loved!

Nineteen years without one faint shadow of love is mouldy, crumbling age—is gray with the dust of centuries.

How long have I lived?

How long must I live?

I am shrieking at you, cold, stupid world.

Oh, the long, long waiting!

The millions of human beings!

I am a human being and there is no one— no one—no one.

Who can know this that has not felt it? You do not know—you can not know.

Surely I do not ask too much. But whether or not it is too much I can not go through the years without it—oh, I can not!

You have lived your nineteen years, fine world, and you have lived through some after years.

But in your nineteen years there was some one to love you.

It is that that counts.

Since you have had that some one, in your nineteen years, can you understand what life is to me—me—in my loneliness?

My wailing, waiting soul burns with but one desire: *to be loved-oh, to be loved.*

I AM making the world my confessor in this Portrayal. My mind is fairly bursting with egotism and pain, and in writing this I find a merciful outlet. I have become fond of my Portrayal. Often I lay my forehead and my lips caressingly upon the pages.

And I wish to let you know that there is in existence a genius—an unhappy genius, a genius starving in Montana in the barrenness—but still a genius. I am a creature the like of which you have never before happened upon. You have never suspected that there is such a person. I know that there is not such another. As I said in the beginning, the world contains not my parallel.

I am a fantasy—an absurdity—a genius!

Had I been one of the beasts that perish I had been likewise a fantasy. I think I should have been a small animal composite of a pig, a leopard, and a skunk: an animal that I fancy would be uncanny to look upon but admirable for a pet.

However, I am not one of the beasts that perish.

I am human.

That is another remarkable point.

I have heard persons say they can hardly believe I am quite human.

I am the most human creature that ever was placed on the earth. The geniuses are always more human than the herd. Almost a perfection of humanness is reached in me. This by itself makes me extraordinary. The rarest thing in the world, I find, is the quality of humanness.

Humanity and humaneness are much less rare.

"It is a brave thing to understand something of what we see." Indeed it is. An exceeding brave thing. The one who said that had surely gone out on the highways and byways and found how little he could understand.

To understand oneself is not so brave a thing. To go in among the hidden gray shadows of the deep things is a fool's errand. It is not from choice that I do it. No one carries a mill-stone around her neck from choice. When I see what is among the hidden gray shadows—when I see a vision of *Myself*—I am seized with a strange, sick terror.

A fool's errand—but one that I must need go—and for that matter I myself am a fool.

Yet to know oneself well is a rare fine art.

I analyze myself now. I analyzed myself when I was three years old.

The only difference is that at the age of three I was not aware that I analyzed. It is true, that is a great difference. Now I know that I am analyzing at nineteen, and now I know that I analyzed at three.

And at the age of nineteen I know that I am a genius.

A genius who does not know that he is a genius is no genius. A drunken man might stagger up to a piano and accidentally play music that vibrates to the soul—that touches upon the mysteries. But he does not know his power, and he is no genius, though men awaken and go mad therefrom.

I know that I am a genius more than any genius that has lived.

I have a feeling that the world will never know this.

And as I think of it I wonder if angels are not weeping somewhere because of it.

"She only said: 'My life is dreary,
    He cometh not,' she said;
She said, 'I am aweary, aweary,
    I would that I were dead!'"

ALL day long this heart-sickening song of Mariana has been reeling and swimming in my brain. I awoke with it early in the morning, and it is still with me now in the lateness. I wondered at times during the day why that very gentle and devilishly persistent refrain did not drive me insane or send me into convulsions. I tried vainly to fix my mind on a book. I began reading "Mill on the Floss," but that weird poem was not to be foiled. It bewitched my brain. Now, as I write, I hear twenty voices chanting in a sad minor key—twenty voices that fill my brain with sound to the bursting point. "He cometh not—he cometh not—he cometh not." "That I were dead"—"I am aweary, aweary,—"that I were dead—that I were dead." "He cometh not—that I were dead."

It is maddening in that it is set sublimely to the music of my own life.

Now that I have written it I can hope that it may leave me. If it follows me through the night, and if I awake to another day of it the cords of my over-worked mind will surely break.

But let me thank the kind Devil.

It is leaving me now!

It is as if tons were lifted from my brain.

HOW can any one bring a child into the world and not wrap it round with a certain wondrous tenderness that will stay with it always!

There are persons whose souls have never entered into them.

My mother has some fondness for me—for my body because it came of hers. That is nothing—nothing.

A hen loves its egg.

A hen!

THIS evening in the slow-deepening dusk I sat by my window and spent an hour in passionate conversation with the Devil. I fancied I sat, with my hands folded and my feet crossed, on an ugly but comfortable red velvet sofa in some nondescript room.

And the fascinating man-devil was seated near in a frail willow chair.

He had willingly come to pass the time of day with me. He was in a good-humored mood, and I amused and interested him. And for myself, I was extremely glad to see the Devil sitting there and felt vividly as always. But I sat quietly enough.

The fascinating man-devil has fascinating steel-gray eyes, and they looked at me with every variety of glance—from quizzical to tender.

It were easy—oh, how easy—to follow those eyes to the earth's ends.

The Devil leaned back in the frail willow chair and looked at me.

"And now that I am here, Mary MacLane," he said, "what would you?"

"I want you to marry me," I replied at once. "And I want it more than ever anything was wanted since the world began."

"So? I am flattered," said the Devil, and smiled gently, enchantingly.

At that smile I was ravished and transported, and a spasm of some rare emotion thrilled all the little nerves in me from my heels to my forehead. And yet the smile was not for me but rather somewhat at my expense.

"But," he went on, "you must know it is not my custom to marry women."

"I am sure it is not," I agreed, "and I do not ask to be peculiarly favored. Anything that you may give me, however little, will constitute marriage for me."

"And would marriage itself be so small a thing?" asked the Devil.

"Marriage," I said, "would be a great, oh, a wonderful thing, and the most beautiful of all. I want what is good according to my lights, and because I am a genius my lights are many and far-reaching."

"What do your lights tell you?" the man-devil inquired.

"They tell me this: that nothing in the world matters unless love is with it, and if love is with it and it seems to the virtuous a barren and infamous thing, still—because of the love—it partakes of the very highest."

"And have you the courage of your convictions?" he said.

"If you offered me," I replied, "that which to the blindly virtuous seems the worst possible thing, it would yet be for me the red, red line on the sky, my heart's desire, my life, my rest. You are the Devil. I have fallen in love with you."

"I believe you have," said the Devil. "And how does it feel to be in love?"

Sitting composedly on the ugly red velvet sofa, with my hands folded and my feet crossed, I attempted to define that wonderful feeling.

"It feels," I said, "as if sparks of fire and ice crystals ran riot in my veins with my blood; as if a thousand pinpoints pierced my flesh, and every other point a point of pleasure, and every other point a point of pain; as if my heart were laid to rest in a bed of velvet and cotton-wool but kept awake by sweet violin arias; as if milk and honey and the blossoms of the cherry flowed into my stomach and then vanished utterly; as if strange, beautiful worlds lay spread out before my eyes, alternately in dazzling light and complete darkness with chaotic rapidity; as if orris-root were sprinkled in the folds of my brain; as if sprigs of dripping-wet sweet-fern were stuck inside my hot linen collar; as if— well, you know," I ended suddenly.

"Very good," said the Devil. "You are in love. And you say you are in love with me."

"Oh, with you!" I exclaimed with suppressed violence. The effort to suppress this violence cost me pounds of nerve-power. But I kept my hands still quietly folded and my feet crossed, and it was a triumph of self-control. "I want you to marry me," I added despairingly.

"And you think," he inquired, "that apart from the opinion of the wise world, it would be a suitable marriage?"

"A suitable marriage!" I exclaimed. "I hate a suitable marriage! No, it would not be suitable. It would be Bohemian, outlandish, adorable!"

The Devil smiled.

This time the smile was for me. And, oh, the long, old, overpowering enchantment of the smile of steel-gray eyes!—the steel-gray eyes of the Devil!

It is one of those things that one remembers.

"You are a beautifully frank, little feminine creature," he said. "Frankness is in these days a lost art."

"Yes, I am beautifully frank," I replied. "Out of countless millions of the Devil's anointed I am one to acknowledge myself."

"But withal you are not true," said the man-devil.

"I am a liar," I answered.

"You are a liar, surely," he said, "but you stay with your lies. To stay with anything is Truth."

"It is so," I replied. "Nevertheless I am false as woman can be."

"But you know what you want."

"Oh, yes," I said, "I know what I want. I want you to marry me."

"And why?"

"Because I love you."

"That seems an excellent reason, certainly," said the Devil.

"I want to be happy for once in my life," I said. "I have never been happy. And if I could be happy once for one gold day, I should be satisfied, and I should have that to remember in the long years."

"And you are a strangely pathetic little animal," said the Devil.

"I am pathetic," I said. I clasped my hands very tightly. "I know that I am pathetic: and for this reason I am the most terribly pathetic of all in the world."

"Poor little Mary MacLane!" said the Devil. He leaned toward me. He looked at me with those strange, wonderfully tender, divine steel-gray eyes. "Poor little Mary MacLane!" he said again in a voice that was like the Gray Dawn. And the eyes—the glance of the steel-gray eyes entered into me and thrilled me through and through. It frightened and soothed me. It racked and comforted me. It ravished me with inconceivable gentleness so that I bent my head down and sobbed as I breathed.

"Don't you know, you little thing," said the man-devil, softly-compassionate, "your life will be very hard for you always—harder when you are happy than when you go in Nothingness?"

"I know—I know. Nevertheless I want to be happy," I sobbed. I felt a rush of an old thick, heavy anguish. "It is day after day. It is week after week. It is month after month. It is year after year. It is only time going and going. There is no joy. There is no lightness of heart. It is only the passing of days. I am young and all alone. Always I have been alone: when I was five and lay in the damp grass and tortured myself to keep back tears; and through the long, cold, lonely years till now—and now all the torture does not keep back the tears. There is no one—nothing—to help me bear it. It is more than pathetic when one is nineteen in all young, new feeling and sees Nothing anywhere— except long, dark, lonely years behind her and before her. No one that loves me and long, long years."

I stopped. The gray eyes were fixed on me. Oh, they were the steel-gray eyes!—and they had a look in them. The long, bitter pageant of my Nothingness mingled with this look and the coming together of these was like the joining of two halves.

I do not know which brings me the deeper pain—the loneliness and weariness of my sand and barrenness, or the look in the steel-gray eyes. But as always I would gladly leave all and follow the eyes to the world's end. They are like the sun's setting. And they are like the pale, beautiful stars. And they are like the shadows of earth and sky that come together in the dark.

"Why," asked the Devil, "are you in love with me?"

"You know so much—so much," I answered. "I think it must be that. The wisdom of the spheres is in your brain. And so, then, you must understand me. Because no one understands all these smouldering feelings my greatest agony is. You must need know the very finest of them. And your eyes! Oh, it's no matter why I'm in love with you. It's enough that I am. And if you married me I would make you happier than you are."

"I am not happy at all," said the man-devil. "I am merely contented."

"Contentment," I said, "in place of Happiness, is a horrid feeling. Not one of your countless advocates loves you. They all serve you faithfully and well, but with it all they hate you. Always people hate their tyrant. You are my tyrant, but I love you absorbingly, madly. Happiness for me would be to live with you and see you made happy by the overwhelming flood of my love."

"It interests me," he said. "You are a most interesting feminine philosopher—and your philosophy is after my own heart, in its lack of *virtue*. It is to be hoped you are not 'intellectual,' which is an unpardonable trait."

"Indeed, I am not," I replied. "Intellectual people are detestable. They have pale faces and bad stomachs and bad livers, and if they are women their corsets are sure to be too tight, and probably black, and if they are men they are *soft*, which is worse. And they never by any chance know what it means to walk all day in the rain, or to roll around on the ground in the dirt. And, above all, they never fall in love with the Devil."

"They are tiresome," the Devil agreed. "If I were to marry you how long would you be happy?"

"For three days."

"You are wise," he said. "You are wonderfully wise in some things, though you are still very young."

"I am wise," I answered. "Being of womankind and nineteen years, I am more than ready to give up absolutely everything that is good in the world's sight, though they are contemptible things enough in my own, for love.

All for love. Therefore I am wise. Also I am a fool."

"Why are you a fool?"

"Because I am a genius."

"Your logic is good logic," said the Devil.

"My logic—oh, I don't care anything about logic," I said with sudden complete weariness. I felt buried and wrapped round and round in weariness. Everything lost its color. Everything turned cold.

"At this moment," said the Devil, "you feel as if you cared for nothing at all. But if I chose I could bring about a transfiguration. I could kiss your soul into Paradise."

I answered, "Yes," without emotion.

"An hour," said the Devil, "is not very long. But we know it is long enough to suffer in, and go mad in, and live in, and be happy in. And the world contains a great many hours. Now I am leaving you. It is likely that I may never come again, and it is likely that I may come again."

It all vanished. I still sat by my window in the gloom. "It is dreary," I said.

But yes. The world contains a great many hours.

I HAVE asked for bread, sometimes, and I have been given a stone.

Oh, it is a bitter thing—oh, it is piteous, piteous!

I find that I am not far apart from human beings I can still be crushed, wounded, stunned, by the attitude of human beings.

To-day I looked for human-kindness, and I was given coldness. I repelled human beings.

I asked for bread and I was given a stone.

Oh, it is bitter—bitter.

Oh, is there a thing in the wide world more bitter?

God, where are you! I am crushed, wounded, stunned—and, oh—I am alone!

I HAVE a sense of humor that partakes of the divine in life—for there are things even in this chaotic irony that are divine. My genius is not divine. My patheticness is not divine. My philosophy is not divine, nor my originality, nor my audacity of thought. These are peculiarly of the earth. But my sense of humor—

It is humor that is far too deep to admit of laughter. It is humor that makes my heart melt with a high, unequaled sense of pleasure and ripple down through my body like old yellow wine.

A rare tone in a person's voice, a densely wrathful expression in a pair of slate-colored eyes, a fine, fine shade of comparison and contrast between a word in a conversation and an angleworm pattern in a calico dressing-jacket—these are things that make me conscious of divine emotion.

One day last summer an Italian peddler-woman stopped at the back door and rested herself. I stood in the doorway, and the peddler-woman and I talked. She had a dirty white handkerchief tied over her head—as all Italian peddler-women do—and she had a telescope valise filled with garters, and hairpins, and soap, and combs, and pencils, and china buttons on blue cards, and bean-shooters, and tacks, and dream-books, and mouth-organs, and green glass beads, and jews-harps. There is something fascinating about a peddler-woman's telescope valise. This peddler-woman wore a black satine wrapper and an ancient cape. She said that she would like to stop and rest a while, and I told her she might. I had always wanted to talk to a peddler-woman, and my mother never would allow one in the house.

"Is it nice to be a peddler?" I asked her.

"It ain't bad," replied the peddler-woman.

"Do you make a great deal of money?" I next inquired.

"Sometime I do, and sometime I don't," said the woman. She spoke with an accent that, while it sounded Italian, still showed unmistakably that she had lived in Butte.

"Well, do you make just enough to live on, or have you saved some money?" I asked.

"I got four hundred dollar in the bank," she replied. "I been peddlin' eight year."

"Eight years of tramping around in all kinds of weather," I said. "Your philosophy must be peripatetic, too. Haven't you ever had rheumatism in your knees?"

"I got rheumatism in every joint in my body," said the woman. "I have to lay off, sometime."

"Have you a husband?" I wished to know.

"I had a man—oh, yes," said the peddler-woman.

"And where is he?"

"Back home-in Italy."

"Why doesn't he come out here and work for you?" I asked.

"Yes, w'y don't he?" said the woman. "Dat-a man, he's dem lucky w'en he can get enough to eat—he is."

"Why don't you send him some money to pay his way out, since you've saved so much?" I inquired.

"Holy God!" said the peddler-woman. "I work hard for dat-a money. I save ev'ry cent. I ain't go'n now to t'row it away—I ain't. Dat-a man, he's all right w'ere he is—he is."

"What did you marry him for?" I asked.

The peddler-woman looked at me with that look which seems to convey the information that curiosity once killed a cat.

"What for?" I persisted—"for love?"

"I marry him w'en I was young girl. And he was young, too."

"Yes—but what did you do it for? Was he awfully nice, and did he say awfully sweet things to you?"

"He was dem sweet—oh, yes," said the peddler-woman. She grinned. "And I was young."

"And you liked it when you were young and he was sweet, didn't you?"

"Yes, I guess so. I was young," she answered.

The fact that one is young seems to imply—in the Italian peddler mind—a lacking in some essential points.

"And don't you like your man now?" I asked.

"Dat-a man, he's all right, in Italy—he is, replied the woman.

"Well," I observed, "if I had a man who had been dem sweet once, when I had been young, but who was not sweet any more, I think I should leave him in Italy, too."

"You'll git a man some day soon," said the peddler-woman.

I was interested to know that.

"They all do—oh, yes," she said.

"But you likely to be better off peddlin', I tell you."

"Yes, I think it would be amusing to be a peddler for a while," I said. "But I should want the man, too, as long as he was dem sweet."

The peddler-woman picked up the telescope valise.

"Yes," she remarked, "a man, he's sweet two days, t'ree days, then—holy God! he never work, he git- a drunk, he make-a rough-house, he raise hell."

The peddler-woman nodded at me and limped out of the yard. The telescope valise was heavy. When she walked every muscle in her body seemed to be pressed into the service. She had a heavy, solid look. She seemed as though she might weigh three hundred pounds, though she was not large. The afternoon sun shone down brightly on her dirty white handkerchief, on her brown comely face, on her brown brass-ringed hands, on her black satine wrapper, on her ancient cape.

As I watched her out of sight I thought to myself: "Two days, t'ree days, then—holy God! he never work, he git-a drunk, he make-a rough-house, he raise hell."

I was conscious of an intense humor that was so far beyond laughter that it was too deep even for tears. But I felt tears vaguely as I watched the peddler-woman limping up the road.

It was not pathos. It was humor—humor. My emotion was one of vivid pleasure—pleasure at the sight of the woman, and at the telescope valise, and at her conversation supplemented by my own.

This emotion is divine, and I can not grasp it.

As I looked after the Italian peddler-woman it came to me with sudden force that the earth is only the earth, but that it is touched here and there brilliantly with divine fingers.

Long and often as I've sat in intense silent passion and gazed at the red, red sunset sky, I have never then felt this sense of the divine.

It comes only through humor.

It comes only with things like an Italian peddler-woman in a black satine wrapper and an ancient cape.

My soul—how heavily it goes.

Life is a journeying up a spring-time hill. And at the top we wonder why we are there. Have mercy on me, I implore in a dull idea that the journey is so long—so long, and a human being is less than an atom.

The solid, heavy figure of an Italian peddler-woman with a telescope valise, limping away in the afternoon sunshine, is more convincing of the Things that Are than would be the sound of the wailing of legions of lost souls, could it be heard.

For the world must be amused.

And the world's wind listeth as it bloweth.

I WRITE a great many letters to the dear anemone lady. I send some of them to her and others I keep to read myself. I like to read letters that I have written—particularly that I have written to her.

This is a letter that I wrote two days ago to my one friend:

"To you:

"And don't you know, my dearest, my friendship with you contains other things? It contains infatuation, and worship, and bewitchment, and idolatry, and a tiny altar in my soulchamber whereon is burning sweet incense in a little dish of blue and gold.

"Yes, all of these.

"My life is made up of many outpourings. All the outpourings have one point of coming-together. You are the point of coming-together. There is no other.

"You are the anemone lady.

"You are the one whom I may love.

"To think that the world contains one beautiful human being for me to love!

"It is wonderful.

"My life is longing for the sight of you. My senses are aching for lack of an anemone to diffuse itself among them.

"A year ago, when you were in the high school, often I used to go over there when you would be going home, so that my life could be made momentarily replete by the sight of you. You didn't know I was there—only a few times when I spoke to you.

"And now it is that I remember you.

"Oh, my dearest—you are the only one in the world!

"We are two women. You do not love me, but I love you.

"You have been wonderfully, beautifully kind to me.

"You are the only one who has ever been kind to me.

"There is something delirious in this—something of the nameless quantity.

"It is old grief and woe to live nineteen years and to remember no person ever to have been kind. But what is it—do you think?—at the end of nineteen years, to come at last upon one who is wonderfully, beautifully kind!

"Those persons who have had some one always to be kind to them can never remotely imagine how this feels.

"Sometimes in these spring days when I walk miles down into the country to the little wet gulch of the sweet-flags, I wonder why it is that this thing does not make me happy. 'She is wonderfully, beautifully kind,' I say to myself—'and she is the anemone lady. She is *wondrously* kind, and though she's gone, nothing can ever change that.'

"But I am not happy.

"Oh, my one friend—what is the matter with me? What is this feeling? Why am I not happy?

"But how can you know?

"You are beautiful.

"I am a small, vile creature.

"Always I awake to this fact when I think of the anemone lady.

"I am not good.

"But you are kind to me—you are kind to me—you are kind to me.

"You have written me two letters.

"The anemone lady came down from her high places and wrote me two letters.

"It is said that God is somewhere. It may be so.

"But God has never come down from his high places to write me two letters.

"Dear—do you see?—you are the only one in the world.

"MARY MACLANE."

O H, THE dreariness, the Nothingness! Day after day—week after week,—it is dull and gray and weary. It is *dull*, DULL, DULL!

No one loves me the least in the world.

"My life is dreary—he cometh not." I am unhappy—unhappy.

It rains. The blue sky is weeping. But it is not weeping because I am unhappy.

I hate the blue sky, and the rain, and the wet ground, and everything. This morning I walked far away over the sand, and these things made me think they loved me—and that I loved them. But they fooled me. Everything fools. me. I am a fool.

No one loves me. There are people here. But no one loves me—no one understands—no one cares.

It is I and the barrenness. It is I—young and all alone.

Pitiful Heaven!—but no, Heaven is not pitiful.

Heaven also has fooled me, more than once.

There is something for every one that I have ever known—some tender thing. But what is there for me? What have I to remember out of the long years?

The blue sky is weeping, but not for me. The rain is persistent and heavy as damnation.

It falls on my mind and it maddens my mind. It falls on my soul and it hurts my soul.—Everything hurts my soul.—It falls on my heart and it warps the wood in my heart.

Of womankind and nineteen years, a philosopher of the peripatetic school, a thief, a genius, a liar, and a fool—and unhappy, and filled with anguish and hopeless despair. What is my life? Oh, what is there for me!

There has always been Nothing. There will always be Nothing.

There was a miserable, damnable, wretched, lonely childhood. Itself has passed, but the pain of it has not passed. The pain of it is with me and is added to the pain of now. It is pain that never lets itself be forgotten. The pain of the childhood was the pain of Nothing. The pain of now is the pain of Nothing. Oh, the pathetic burlesque-tragedy of Nothing!

It is burlesque, but it is none the less tragedy. It is tragedy that eats its way inward.

It is only I and the sand and barrenness.

I have never a tender thing in my life. The sand and barrenness has never a grass-blade.

I want a human being to love me. I have need of it. I am starving to death for lack of it.

Bitterest salt tears surge upward—sobs are shaking themselves out from the depths. Oh, the salt is bitter. I might lay me down and weep all day and all night—and the salt would grow more bitter and more bitter.

But life in its Nothingness is more bitter still.

It is burlesque-tragedy that is the most tragic of all.

It is an inward dying that never ends. It is the bitterness of death added to the bitterness of life.

What hell is there like that of one weak little human being placed on the earth—and left *alone?*

There are people who live and enjoy. But my soul and I—we find life too bitter, and too heavy to carry alone. Too bitter, and too heavy.

Oh, that I and my soul might perish at this moment, forever!

I AM sitting writing out on my sand and barrenness. The sky is pale and faded now in the west, but a few minutes ago there was the same old-time, always-new miracle of roses and gold, and glints and gleams of silver and green, and a river in vermilions and purples—and lastly the dear, the beautiful: the red, red line.

There also are heavy black shadows.

I have given my heart into the keeping of this.

And still, as always, I look at it—and feel it all with thrilling passion—and await the Devil's coming.

L'ENVOI:

October 28, 1901.

AND so there you have my Portrayal. It is the record of three months of Nothingness. Those three months are very like the three months that preceded them, to be sure, and the three that followed them—and like all the months that have come and gone with me, since time was. There is never anything different; nothing ever happens.

Now I will send my Portrayal into the wise wide world. It may stop short at the publisher; or it may fall stillborn from the press; or it may go farther, indeed, and be its own undoing.

That's as may be.

I will send it.

What else is there for me, if not this book?

And, oh, that some one may understand it!

—I am not good. I am not virtuous. I am not sympathetic. I am not generous. I am merely and above all a creature of intense passionate *feeling*. I feel—everything. It is my genius. It burns me like fire.

My Portrayal in its analysis and egotism and bitterness will surely be of interest to some. Whether to that one alone who may understand it; or to some who have themselves been left alone; or to those three whom I, on three dreary days, asked for bread, and who each gave me a stone—and whom I do not forgive (for that is the bitterest thing of all): it may be to all of these.

But none of them, nor any one, can know the feeling made of relief and pain and despair that comes over me at the thought of sending all this to the wise wide world. It is bits of my wooden heart broken off and given away. It is strings of amber beads taken from the fair neck of my soul. It is shining little gold coins from out of my mind's red leather purse. It is my little old life-tragedy.

It means everything to me.

Do you see?—it means *everything* to me.

It will amuse you. It will arouse your interest. It will stir your curiosity. Some sorts of persons will find it ridiculous. It will puzzle you.

But am I to suppose that it will also awaken compassion in cool, indifferent hearts? And will the sand and barrenness look so unspeakably gray and dreary to coldly critical eyes as to mine? And shall my bitter little story fall easily and comfortably upon undisturbed ears, and linger for an hour, and be forgotten?

Will the wise wide world itself give me in my outstretched hand a stone?

THE END

Want to know more about the rip-roaring town where Mary MacLane grew up?

Here are the two best books about Butte, Montana, during its spectacular mining years.

Copper Camp
The Lusty Story of Butte, Montana, the Richest Hill on Earth
By the Writers Project of Montana
336 pages, 25 photos
$19.95, ISBN 1-931832-04-8

Copper Camp describes the eccentric citizens of Butte during the late 1800s and early 1900s when Butte was high, wide, and wide-open. According to the book's introduction, "Here are the kids and characters, ministers, miners, mothers, girls from the line, bankers, and barkeeps. Of such stuff as strikes, parades, politics and people—above all, of rawboned, lively, honest-to-God people—is a mining camp composed; and Butte, in the opinion of many experts, is *the* mining camp."

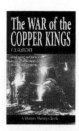

The War of the Copper Kings
By C. B. Glasscock
320 pages, photographs
$19.95, ISBN 1-931832-21-8

Greed, corruption, bribery, fraud—insiders getting fabulously rich while workers get robbed. Sound familiar? This was Butte, Montana, at the dawn of the twentieth century. Three men of vastly different backgrounds fought for Butte's mineral wealth with greed and generosity, cruelty and compassion, cowardice and courage. *The War of the Copper Kings* is the best account of this brazen battle for wealth and power, a story of raw human drama and timeless historical significance.

RIVERBEND
PUBLISHING